GREYHOUND TALES

From Route 66

First published as

BEHIND THE WHEEL

On Route 66

Written & Illustrated
by
Howard Suttle

Data Plus! Printing and Publishing
Raton, New Mexico

First Edition October 1996
Behind The Wheel on Route 66

Illustrations by
Howard Suttle
Editors: Ms.Joan MacNeish and Ms.Linda Johnson

Published by
Data Plus! Printing and Publishing
A Division of Lusk Industries

Printed in the United States by
Western Christian Foundation
Wichita Falls, Texas

Copyright 1993 by Howard Suttle

* * * * *

Second Edition March 2004
Greyhound Tales From Route 66

From Coda Publications
P.O.B. 71, Raton, NM 87740

All correspondence, orders and inquiries should be directed to
Coda Publications
P.O.B. 71, Raton, New Mexico 87740 U.S.A.

ISBN 0-910390-01-0
Library of Congress Card Catalog Number 96-71236

**Published in Raton by
Coda Publications
P.O.B. 71, Raton, NM 87740 U.S.A.**

FOREWORD

The time has come for the over-the-road bus driver of America to have a few moments in the sun. Howard Suttle has lived the life, written the words and drawn the pictures that will do just that. Howard did it all for Greyhound, our most famous bus company, on U.S. Highway 66, our most famous highway. His stories range from small laughs to huge tragedies. They all say much about buses and the people who drive and ride them, but also much about the human condition and spirit.

There was a time when small boys dreamed of growing up to be like Howard Suttle, to be a bus driver, to be the captain of those glorious blue and silver, red and cream machines that sped passengers to destinations from here to the other side of the country or the county. For the most part, changes in the bus business and the little boy dream business have done away with those dreams.

Howard may bring them back. I hope so.

Jim Lehrer
Host of "The News Hour"
on PBS

PREFACE

It was 1951, only a few months after starting my driving career of twenty-eight years with Greyhound. As I sat at road-side rest stop, having coffee and telling a fellow driver about some incident that happened on old Route 66, he told me that I should keep notes and someday, I might want to write a book. Laughing, I said, "Me? A book?" I had needed help just to fill out my application. I told him that if I was lucky enough to reach the age of sixty-six, I might do just that.

Well, it seems to me now that this little conversation took place only a short time ago; but, as I write this, it seems kind of odd that I am now, indeed, sixty-six years of age. Up until this time, I have been very uninterested in attempting such a thing. But, after looking back down the road two and a half million miles, I have decided to share some of these true stories. Realizing that only a few family members and friends might be interested in the least; nevertheless, it makes me feel good to share some of the experiences of the old road called Route 66.

I've seen every emotion displayed that's humanly possible: temper, rage, jealousy, selfishness, greed. Some were brought on by drunkenness, drugs, and other misfortunes of the human spirit. The one emotion I would like to acknowledge far above all the rest is a four-letter word called "love". It is so mysterious that it simply cannot be explained by an old ex-bus driver. Still, I would like to thank all of the people whom I have seen display it so freely back through the years. Especially, I thank the older drivers and Greyhound personnel who helped me in so many ways that they can't be counted. The unforgettable thing about this is the fact that most of them have gone over the hill--and I now realize that I waited too long to tell them so.

Also, I thank every passenger who rode with me whom I didn't have the time to personally acknowledge. My thanks to the ladies who helped young mothers with their babies during the times we were stuck in blizzards with little food. My thanks, also, to the truck drivers who worked so diligently to shovel the bus out of snow drifts so the women and children could get to town.

To the people who generously gave of their money when an elderly gentleman lost his wallet and felt all alone, I give my thanks. To the kind people who picked me up from the side of the road every time the bus broke down, and other countless unselfish people with whom I have had the pleasure of coming in contact, my thanks seem inadequate.

Surely, my family knows how much I appreciate their cooperation by helping me hold down this job of irregular hours, by allowing me to sleep during the day, and the many other countless acts of unselfish love. I appreciate the spirit of my son, who couldn't depend on his father to be at school functions like normal folks--his dad was running Route 66.

Realizing many people couldn't care less about history, I feel that if only one person who reads this learns the lesson of 'love', it will be well worth the effort. I once overheard two elderly gentlemen talking on the front seat one night shortly after the death of millionaire, Howard Hughes. One asked the other, "I wonder how much money Howard Hughes left?" I'll always remember the other fellow's answer, which fairly sums up the meaning of life. He said, "I imagine he left all of it." How true! This serves to remind me of the saying that 'You can only enjoy what you give to others. Love thy neighbor.'

Howard Suttle

DEDICATION

Dedication of these true-life experiences is to all of the fine men and women who took the time to show me and teach me the know-how of becoming a bus driver; people who had experienced the old days of bad roads, no air conditioning, no rest rooms, and few of the modern-day conveniences. They had to endure the depression era, wartime, and many adverse conditions to transport millions of Americans from all walks of life to and from jobs, college, the army, etc., and who took care of their families waiting at home for their husband and father, who drove hundreds of miles--on solid ice, at times (and maybe as much as twenty-four hours late)--but kept the faith.

To all of these fine people, whether still living or deceased, and to new drivers: if for a minute you think your job is unimportant, let me remind you that you alone are in charge in case of trouble. While I have great admiration for the airline industry, you must remember that they have several on board in case of trouble. They have two-way communication, control people on the ground, federal marshals riding at times, and many other advantages. Even the driver of the eighteen-wheelers has the old reliable CB and he can smoke a cigar, sing, or whistle while driving; he can talk to his buddies or listen to his favorite singer on his cassette.

The bus driver must sit there with both hands on the wheel; no smoking, no drinking of coffee or any other beverage, no form of entertainment--not even a little radio with an ear plug--and drive for hours, with one eye on the road and one eye on the passenger mirror. He must drive on ice, through fog, sand, snow, and sleet--so little grandmother or college student can get to their destination.

Be proud. You are doing the job of several people and you are all alone. To all of you, these stories are truly dedicated.

Howard Suttle

AND NOW...IN SUMMARY

As I write these true stories, I try to remember when certain things happened, but to no avail. As these accounts were unfolding, writing a book about them was the farthest thing from my mind. Consequently, the exact dates of these events were not recorded.

I can't recall either, the exact time that every town along Route 66 was by-passed by the interstates, because not all sections were completed at the same time. There was a period of time that both old Route 66 and the new interstate were used. In fact, back then, we were relieved to get the privilege of using the new road. In more recent years, as Greyhound obtained more modern equipment and more of the interstate was completed, we started more express schedules and the smaller places were by-passed. Times were a'changin' indeed!! As we traveled the new road in more modern buses (with restrooms, etc.), we could see the smaller places like Glen Rio, Cuervo, Newkirk, and numerous other places slowly deteriorate and start to look like ghost towns.

After retirement, my wife and I made a trip to California by auto. As we left Amarillo, heading west, I was reminded of old Route 66 since the old road is still used in some places. While continuing west into New Mexico, you can see the old road in several places, if you know where to look. In fact, all the way through New Mexico, I was constantly reminded of its presence. From the central part of the state to Albuquerque, there are still a lot of reminders of times past. Through Arizona, its presence is felt and seen in many places.

After spending the night in Arizona, we continued west on the interstate. After leaving Needles, en route to Barstow, I couldn't help but wonder how those old, crude cars with poor tires, no air conditioning, and bad roads with little water and lots of dust and heat ever made it. I often wondered how many dreams that old desert crushed. As we traveled on through the San Bernardino Mountains and into Los Angeles, the thought of an entire family working its way out here in an old jalopy must have been frightening, to say the least.

Leaving LA, we continued up the coast to Carmel, Monterey, Salinas, then back to Bakersfield and east toward Amarillo. I couldn't help but wonder just how many of the prosperous farmers and vineyard operators could trace the routes of their ance stors back down old Route 66. About that time, I could see jet trails crisscrossing the sky. Times, indeed, are still a' changin'.

As far as the times being better, I don't know...but one thing I know for sure: as long as man is alive and kickin', he will continue to push ahead full-speed into future realms unknown, for this is the nature of man. But just as old Route 66 will fade into the past, along with the wagon ruts and the stage coach, so some day, the jet airliner will give way to some other form of transportation.

But, at least for a while, we can still look over at the old road, (and in some cases, actually drive on it) and remember how it once was...for someday, not too far into the future, these tracks will also fade into history.

Howard Suttle

THE STORIES

Meeting My Future Wife	1
The Application	5
First Week of Drivers' School	9
Now We Start Driving	13
The Good-Natured Canadians	17
200 Miles Per Hour	21
Bus Left Without a Driver	25
The Frightened Lady	29
A Small Voice	33
He Loves Cigars	39
The Christmas Tree	45
Snowed-in Away From Home	47
The Bus That Wouldn't Die	53
Grandpa's Bedtime	59
A Matter of Interpretation	63
Snow Storm on Adrian Hill	67
The Post Office Robber	71
A Couple of Beers	75
Highway Fatalities	79
The Ladies' Lounge	87
The British Snow Storm	93
Gunnin' for Romeo	99
The Christmas Peanuts	103
The Stinkin' Christmas	107
Dive Bombing	111
One Thousand Cows	115
Anxious Little Old Lady	117
The Driver is a Genius	119
The Vanishing Vodka	125
Where's the Courthouse?	129

Soldiers to St. Louis   133
The Crazy Hop-Head   137
The Big Blizzard   141
Toddler Missing   151
Help from Ole' Bennie   153
Bridge Out at Sayre, Oklahoma   159
The Stately Gentleman Flips Out   161
At Face Value   165
Tied up at Hinton Junction, Oklahoma   169
The Screwtail Puppy   173
Money Laundering   175

MORE STORIES

The Trailways Comedian   179
Lunch for the Trucker   183
Bad Bus Accident at Hydro, Oklahoma   187
Can't Tell by Looking   193
No Anti-Freeze   197
Racing the Baby   199
The Wino   203
The Red Light and White Lie   205
The Dancing Lady   209
Black Ice Christmas   211
Plenty of Time for a Beer   215
The Cricket Invasion   219
The Race is On   221
How Many Fingers?   225
Salt Water Treatment   227
A Tribute to a Big Grinnin' Okie   231
Hank Finds a Jack   235
Seeing Elephants   238

Hippie and His Dog   241
Colored Ride in Back   243
The Midnight Crisis   245
The Navajo and the Rattler   249
Old Hudson Hotel   251
A Big Hug for a Little Lady   255
A Real Live Pluto   259
No Power-Steering   263
The Bifocals   267
A Close Call   271
The Run-Away Engine   273
No Clutch Bus   277
The Domino Player   279
The Old Silverside   283
The Unhappy Trucker   287
Poor Family and No Credit Card   291
The Stowaway   295
The Ticket Punch   299
A Short Nap   303
Wettbacks to El Paso   307
Bag Not Mine   309
Tunnel Vision   311
The Rubber Up-Chuck   313
Can't Go Home for Christmas   317

EVEN MORE STORIES

The Broken Toy   321
More than a Wolf Whistle   325
The One-Eyed Horse   327
Hamburger Etiquette   331
The Would-Be Cowboy   335
The Ballerina   339

THE END

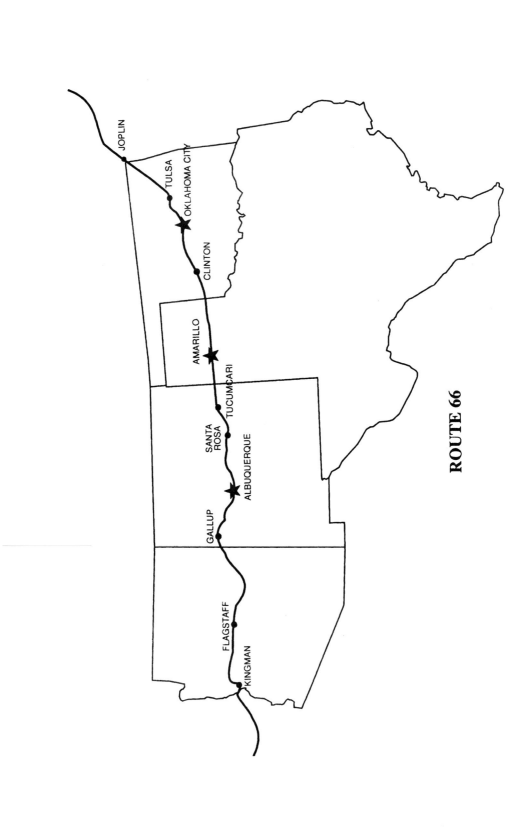

ROUTE 66

MEETING MY FUTURE WIFE

After serving in World War II as tank
commander in the European Theater, I arrived in
Fort Sam Houston, San Antonio, in 1945. I did not
get discharged immediately, as I had received a gun-
shot wound in the right knee, and was due for some
physical therapy, but did manage to get a leave for a
couple of weeks before the therapy. Needless to say,
by going back to my home town of Crosbyton, in full
uniform and on crutches, I was fairly well noticed in
this small, cotton-farming town of less than two
thousand.

While there, I did notice a couple of sisters
that kinda' caught my eye. They were Joyce and
Maxine Hash, who had moved there with their
parents and younger brother a short time earlier
from the big city of Poolville--about a hoot and a
holler west of Ft. Worth. After returning to the base
in San Antonio to await my discharge, I couldn't keep
my thoughts from the older of the sisters. She
walked the town often and would pass my mother's
house. She had long, black hair and dark eyes...and
I thought she would probably be too busy and
popular for the likes of me.

After receiving my discharge from the army,
I moved in with my mother, two older brothers, one
older sister, and two younger sisters. My father had
passed away several years before--leaving my
mother with a whole house full of hungry mouths to
feed. I guess the war did her some good, as it took

1

her three sons away for a while. Luckily, we all came back.

I finally got up my nerve to ask this older sister, Maxine, for a date. It scared the heck out of me when she accepted. We started double dating with Charles Herring and Chris Barrington. The four of us became inseparable and dated constantly. Finally, I married this dark-haired beauty and moved to Amarillo to work with her father, who was in the combine business.

In 1947, we were given a big ole' brown-eyed boy weighing eight and a half pounds. Meanwhile, Charles and Chris had gotten married and were presented with a big, blue-eyed girl. Their birthdays were close together. The Herrings lived in Lubbock.

While working in wheat harvest and many other dead-end jobs, we became close friends with a couple who had moved to Amarillo from east Texas. They were J.D. Williams and his wife, Mavis. J.D. and his brother, Aubry, had obtained a service station. Aubry's wife was Mavis' sister, Maureen. With brothers marrying sisters, I always kidded them about not being allowed too far away from their nest.

One evening in the spring of 1951, J.D. and Mavis came for a visit. Larry, our son, was two years old then and J.D. was constantly teasing him. That night, J.D. asked me if I would like to be a Greyhound bus driver. He had noticed an ad in the paper wanting drivers. After reading the ad, I was discouraged. One of the qualifications was a high-school education, and as I had been drafted for the army, I hadn't finished acquiring one.

My older brother, C. R., was driving for Trailways out of Dallas, and he wanted me to come down and apply with his company. One of their qualifications was to be six feet tall and 185 pounds. I was the runt of the litter and had stopped growing at five feet, eight inches. Also, about the time I discovered that boys and girls were made a little different; my weight stopped at about 140 pounds. It was also about that time that I noticed girls would run when I chased them, so my weight had stayed there. Anyway, this was another reason I was discouraged about trying for Greyhound. However, after another cup of coffee and a few more lies and laughs, J.D. suggest that I try anyway--perhaps the tour in the army would count for something.

THE APPLICATION

After J.D. Williams told me about the ad for Greyhound drivers, I went to the bus station and managed to get an application filled out. After talking with the supervisor, Tom Spillar, I was sent out to a local doctor for a physical. While there, the doctor decided the gun-shot wound in my right knee would not be a problem. As applicants, J.D. and I were told we had to go to a three-week drivers' school in Dallas. We were warned that not all who attended the school would become drivers.

At the time, J.D. was a service writer at the Nash dealership, and his wife worked at Santa Fe Railroad. I worked at a local furniture store, and Maxine was a mother and housewife. So, J.D. decided to take his new Nash Ambassador to Dallas so we would not have to rely on city buses.

The day we reported to the proper people in Dallas, we were given room and board in Oak Cliff, an old rooming-house with army-type bunks and a shared bath. There was no air conditioning, only a ceiling fan--but this was 1951.

That same afternoon, we were to undergo an eye examination and visual coordination test. The following day, we found there were thirty-two of us in this class. The instructor started calling names for those who had failed the exam. Several went forward and were given a bus ticket to return home. I could have swallowed my teeth when the instructor called out J.D. Williams. Seems J.D. was color-blind and I hadn't even known.

5

That night, as I lay in that old bunk in Oak Cliff, hot and sticky, listening to that old ceiling fan clank, I suddenly became quite lonesome. I was already missing my dark-haired beauty and brown-eyed two and half year-old cowboy and was wondering: "What am I doing down here? Probably get washed out anyway." I must have drifted off to sleep, for the next thing I knew, it was time to line up for the shower, get dressed, take a city bus, and report to that big, scary Greyhound institution of higher learning. After all, I had already been rejected by Trailways; what the heck gave me the idea I could become a Greyhound driver? Thinking of all the days I would look up, while growing up in the cotton fields of West Texas, and see the blue and white, shiny and sleek Greyhound (or any other bus) whizzing by on the way to great adventure with destination signs like New York, Dallas, and other far-away places displayed on the front, I remembered my feeling of great admiration and envy of those folks.

Also, I especially noticed the drivers--leaning back, chest out, with a tie on, and that punch! Man, wouldn't it be nice to drive one of those huge monsters full of pretty girls sitting back and watching me and that punch! I'd stand by the door with the engines running, punching tickets, click, click, click. Then I'd put that punch away in that little holster and drive out of this dusty cotton town on the way to Dallas; and I'd make it a point to wave at people working in the cotton patch. About that time, the city bus stopped near the Greyhound station, and I decided, "Boy, this is it; keep your cool, you can do it."

FIRST WEEK OF
DRIVERS' SCHOOL

When we arrived at the Greyhound station, we were ushered upstairs in the terminal building. There were several important-looking officials scattered around, and (once inside the classroom) we were seated at long tables with everyone facing a large blackboard. We were then introduced to several men dressed in slacks, shirts and ties. I thought, "Ties? In Dallas? In early summer? Oh, well."

We were told that, as time went on, several would be dropped from the list of eligibility, no doubt. There were several reasons for this, but it was usually due to falsifying applications concerning arrests, divorce, or any other obvious signs of lying. We were asked if any of us wanted to reconsider our applications before the personnel "head hunter" found out about it. When no one responded, they continued with the business at hand.

The school would consist of two weeks of classroom instruction, the third week would be actual driving. We were issued a Greyhound manual, which covered every situation possible. No doubt, it was based on years of experience and also was to cover their pile, or give them the reason to fire you. After glancing through this manual, I noticed that every situation or subject would end with "Violation will be cause for immediate dismissal."

At five o'clock the first day, we returned to our boarding house in Oak Cliff, talking with fellow students about how guilty we felt for getting thirty-six dollars a week for this. At least some of us could laugh about it.

As I lay on my bunk that night, I again got quite homesick and got the bright idea that perhaps my wife and boy could come to Irving and visit her grandmother who lived alone at that time. If so, I would take the bus to and from there rather than stay in "Cockroach Hotel." After calling Maxine, she agreed to come the following day.

The next day in school went slightly better because my family was on the way down and I looked forward to that. Then, all at once, they called the names of four men to come forward, get a ticket and go home no explanation. This started me wondering whether I had made an unintentional mistake or statement on my application. But five o'clock came without incident, so I caught my bus for Irving and the reunion with my family. After visiting awhile, I started studying the next day's assignment.

The first two weeks consisted of paper work. We covered every word of the driver's manual, waybills, towns printed on a form, etc. For instance, the division I would be working out of would be Amarillo, and I had to memorize every town, crossroad, junction, store or whatever from Amarillo to Oklahoma City, Albuquerque, and Raton, both forwards and backwards. We had written tests on everything: towns, bus models, capacities of buses, fuel, oil, trouble-shooting, maintenance of everything, from buses to personal equipment, accident reports, witness slips and the procedure to follow in every conceivable type of situation. It's amazing how many types of fires we had to know about.

The handling of passengers was very big on the agenda. Oops! Three more were called out and sent home. For those of you who might remember, in 1951, things were still segregated. We were told how to handle the colored passengers. They, according to the law at that time, were told to ride in the rear of the bus. At every station, there were 'white' and 'colored' drinking fountains and restrooms. Every rest stop or bus station had a place for colored people; usually a small table in the rear of the kitchen--never any place with much comfort or dignity.

Finally, I made it through the first two weeks of classroom work--thanks to my wife, who was always very encouraging. She saw to it that I did my homework. Every night when I arrived in Irving, I couldn't get it out of my mind that some more men were sent home. There were thirty-two when we started, and now we were down to eighteen.

NOW WE START DRIVING

Two weeks down and one to go. The third week, as we were divided into three groups of six each, a seasoned driver would take one group, get a bus and take us out to practice 'going through the gears'. We were not allowed to go over thirty-five mph for the first two or three days. Our instructor was Ed Sisk, who had many years of experience and was one of the finest gentlemen I ever worked with. But, as we were about to find out, Ed was by no means a pussy cat. He took us out to the 'ready line' and told one of the men in our group to check out bus number so and so. The rest of us stood by and watched.

The student was to check the oil, fuel card, lights, turn signals, and everything we had been previously instructed to check. One procedure was to 'bump' the rear tires with the baggage crank--at that time the baggage and all other compartments on the bus required a metal crank. The 'bump' was required because with dual tires, if one was flat, you couldn't tell by looking. But by tapping on them, if they were up, they would have a sound kinda' like a ripe watermelon. If one was flat, it would have a mushy thud sound. The student found the rear tires okay and proceeded to bump the front tires. Poor guy! He didn't even realize that if the front tire (being single) was flat, you could tell by looking. Needless to say, we all got a good laugh at the expense of this greenhorn.

After starting the bus, the next very important thing was not to attempt to move the vehicle until the air-gauge read ninety pounds. This was to insure that the brake system would work properly. After the student adjusted the seat and rear-view mirrors, Ed instructed him to proceed out the gate, and turn right on to the street. Since the poor guy had no previous experience with double-clutching, this was to be quite a ride. The buses at that time were four-speed manual and it was important to learn to synchronize the engine RPM with the actual movement of the bus in order to shift gears smoothly. He was told to take a right at the next corner. The fellow got in the right lane, turn-signals on, but the bus was too close to the curb--resulting in quite a shock when he turned. Because he didn't check the right mirror, he ran over the curb.

At that time, Ed told him to pull over and stop the bus. Ed told all of us to be thankful there hadn't been a little old lady standing on that corner. He told the student to take a seat and called the next man. The next day, our group was down to five, as the first student had washed out. The next student was a former truck driver and did fine. We could only go up to thirty-five mph and into third gear for the next day or two.

Our group now consisted of five men, plus Ed. We became sorta' like a family and most of us could drive the bus fairly well. We would leave in the morning, ride around, stop out at Love Field, watch planes, stop for coffee, and...in general...just put in driving time with a lot of goofing off.

There were four students in our group from Abilene, and myself. Since I was from Amarillo and Ed lived in Dallas, Ed decided the last day of school, he might be able to get permission to go to Abilene for some high-speed driving. Also, coming back, we could get in some night driving. It's not known how he did it, but the last morning, he told us we were going to Abilene. The four men from there were quite thrilled, and they could have two hours there. Then we would have to return to Dallas. Ed apologized to me, but since I was the only one from Amarillo, and the distance was so great, he guessed that he and I could loaf for a couple of hours.

One of the Abilene drivers, the one with trucking experience, drove us out of Dallas...still in third gear. When we got on the open road, Ed told him to put it in fourth and take us to Abilene. The student was ready, as we had crept around through the gears for several days. When the driver shifted into fourth and put the old pedal down, we all cheered and had a big laugh. Just hear the wind! Look at the way this old girl slips by those little ole' cars, so smooth and fast, up to seventy per. Now, that was what we had been waiting for! Looking at Ed, who had moved back about half-way in the bus, I could see a slight grin...as if he knew he had something to do with the fact that here were five good Greyhound drivers. Ed just sat there and talked about going fishing as soon as we returned to Dallas. The run to Abilene and the return to Dallas were completed without any problems.

The next morning, we all went to the Texas Department of Public Safety and received our chauffeur's licenses. Man, what a thrill! We'd made it! Now, we felt like real chauffeurs, indeed.

THE GOOD-NATURED CANADIANS

After getting my required rest in Oklahoma City, I was loafing in the hotel lobby waiting for an assignment back to my home base in Amarillo, when the dispatcher called and assigned me to take a bus load of Canadian women to Amarillo. That didn't sound too bad, but when the dispatcher pointed to an old Silversides bus that had no air conditioner, I thought, "Why me, Lord?"

The dispatcher advised me that it was the only bus he had licensed for Texas. It would have to do, and the women would be furnished a newer bus in Amarillo to continue on west, especially across the desert on toward Los Angeles. It was mid-July and you can imagine how hot an old bus can get. " Oh well, beats workin'!" I told myself.

After the ladies finished their rest stop, they loaded up. I stood in front, facing them, dreading to tell them the bad news. They had about five hours of hot riding to do. I couldn't help but notice that this was a group of unusually young women. After telling them the bad news, I was shocked when they started clapping their hands and seemed very pleased. Thinking, at first, that they were playing a joke of some kind on me, one of the ladies on the front seat explained that they liked to open windows so they could take plenty of pictures. In fact, they said they were quite disappointed most of their trip because the buses were too cold and the drivers had discouraged them from opening windows. They couldn't take very good pictures through the tinted windows of the newer buses.

"But what about the heat?" I asked. They didn't think much about it, but one lady suggested they all change into shorts and lighter clothing. So, I opened the baggage door and they used the ladies room to change. After about thirty minutes we were on our way. Leaving town, I've never heard so much laughing and carrying on. It seemed that there was a camera sticking out the windows constantly. I didn't know what they were taking pictures of that was so interesting, but they seemed to enjoy it.

About two hours later, we stopped in Clinton for a rest stop and several of the ladies told me they were having a ball. I couldn't believe it, but they were treating me like some kind of a hero. The old bus didn't have a rest room and I told them we would stop again in Shamrock, in about an hour and a half. Everything went fairly well until we approached Erick, which was about thirty minutes from Shamrock. I noticed the heat indicator had started to buzz, telling me the old engine was overheating. We were taught that in order to make it into the next town, sometimes shifting into a lower gear would relieve the problem.

This I did, and the engine cooled back to normal, but this cut my speed down to about forty-five mph. We finally made it into Erick, and after I checked the water level, we continued on toward Shamrock, using fourth gear (the highest gear back then) and going down hill. We made it there without much more trouble and during the rest stop, I called the shop in Amarillo and was told the water pump had probably gone out. I was told I could run in second and sometimes third and make it okay. We agreed that doing that would probably get us to Amarillo quicker than a relief bus could be sent out since it would take a driver about an hour to report to the shop, another two hours to arrive in Shamrock, and then we'd have to spend the time changing a bus load of luggage.

So, once again, I stood in front and asked for their attention, telling them the bad news about the slow trip to Amarillo. I was amazed when they started clapping again. I told them, "You gotta be kidding!" They were very serious as going slower would give them more time to focus their cameras. From Shamrock to Amarillo took only an additional thirty minutes, so it wasn't too bad, after all. Their attitude turned a bad day into a very enjoyable one, despite the heat and wind.

Boy, wouldn't this old world be a better place to live if everyone could turn their misfortune into an enjoyable experience? After that, I often wondered if they needed any drivers in Canada.

200 MILES PER HOUR

As I left Albuquerque one winter afternoon heading for Amarillo, the sun was shining brightly, but I had noticed that the clouds hanging between the Sandia and Manzano Mountains looked as if they were coming down. The top of the Sandias was already covered with clouds. Earlier we had been advised that the Texas panhandle and the state of Oklahoma were preparing for some nasty weather. As I topped out and started down to Moriarty, the weather had turned to a light, misty rain, but the temperature was warm enough that it was no problem.

We had our evening meal stop at the Club Cafe in Santa Rosa. While eating, Floyd Shaw, one of the owners, told me that people coming from the east were talking of ice. That information didn't help my digestive system. Oh well, poor me, I thought. Maybe I could get to Amarillo before ice starts forming on the highway.

As we loaded up and left Santa Rosa heading east, the weather was about the same...wet, but no ice. Everything was normal as I approached the state line of Texas at Glen Rio, but it was now getting dark, which meant I would have to be cautious about invisible ice. As we had no CB radios, we had to rely on only what we could see. The best way to check on the icy conditions was to watch very closely for mist being kicked up by other vehicles, as well as your own.

Sometimes, if there was not traffic close enough to furnish light, I would touch the brake pedal just enough to activate the stop lights. If moisture and spray were present, this would allow me to see it in the rear-view mirror; but, usually, there was enough traffic to keep track of the spray. Another indicator is ice forming on the side-view mirror, which usually happens before it freezes on the highway.

After passing through the small town of Adrian, about forty-five miles west of Amarillo, I stuck my hand out the window and felt for ice on the mirror. As it was only wet, I returned to full speed of about seventy-two mph. I followed the same procedure at the next town of Vega. As I was only thirty miles from home, I was feeling good about the situation, and continued running along at about 72 mph and had thoroughly convinced myself that the road was okay.

About that time, I noticed a Continental Trailways bus parked out in a pasture, and before this could soak in, I noticed a car with a U-Haul trailer had skidded off the road. Then, on the right side of the road, I noticed a truck had jack-knifed and finally the light came on! The surface of the road had frozen and these drivers were taken by surprise. I thought, "Old buddy, here it is and you got caught with your pants down, too. Poor me!" I began to let off the accelerator ever so slowly, realizing that any sudden action on my part would throw the old girl into a tail-spin. I finally eased my foot completely off the pedal, but it felt like she was going at least two-hundred mph. My palms were sweating because I was holding the wheel so tightly. Literally almost afraid to breathe or even look around for fear of doing something wrong, I looked down at the speedometer. I was still traveling at sixty-five miles per hour, and I started thinking, "Please slow down. Whoa, please slow down, stay straight, slow down!"

It seemed to take forever to get my speed down to where I felt half-way comfortable...which was about three mph. Looking in the passenger mirror, everyone seemed to be sleeping comfortably. Relaxing my grip on the wheel, I noticed I was as tight as a fiddle string. My arm pits were sweaty, as well as my palms. Taking a deep breath and easing back down into the seat while trying to regain some composure, I noticed there was very little traffic; and what there was seemed to be creeping along. Every few hundred yards, I'd notice another vehicle that had spun off the road. Okay, now that I had this thing under control, what was the best way to complete the next twenty miles? My only conclusion was: "Very slowly." I can't recall how long it took me to make it into the station. All I know is that it seemed like forever.

After pulling into the station, the last passenger off was a little old lady who asked me, "Sir, do I change here?" referring to the buses, of course. I told her that she didn't have to, but "No doubt, I would need to." It's a good thing that she didn't know what I meant.

BUS LEFT WITHOUT A DRIVER

One evening, while having our evening meal stop at Santa Rosa, a westbound Scenicruiser pulled up in front of the Club Cafe and stopped. The driver was not on a schedule that had a rest stop there, but was required to stop and check if there were any passengers waiting. As all the other buses there were going east and had filled the parking lot, the driver pulled in front and double-parked for a couple of minutes...which was the standard practice. When he was checking for passengers, he also got a cup of coffee in a Styrofoam cup to take with him. About this time, an employee, having seen this driver get off the bus, asked him if he was the driver of the bus in the street. He said, "Yeah, why?" He was then informed that the bus had just left.

Looking out the door, the driver only saw the tail lights going down the street. Realizing the bus was fully-loaded, the driver threw his coffee down and started chasing the bus. After about four blocks of hard running, the bus finally started rolling to a stop. As he pulled the unlatched door open and dove inside, he found a large woman in the driver's seat with both hands on the wheel. She said to him, "Boy, this thing sure steers easy, don't it?" The driver was sure thankful that she, at least, had the frame of mind to steer the bus.

Upon investigation, these were the facts. The Club Cafe is located about four blocks uphill from the Pecos River Bridge. For reasons unknown, the parking brake had malfunctioned and the bus had started rolling. This lady, who was seated on the front seat, had jumped under the wheel and kept it going straight. As the bus started up the other side of the river, it slowed and then the winded, young driver had caught up with it.

He said that when he asked her if she knew enough to steer, why hadn't she stepped on the brake pedal, she had replied that when she glanced down and saw so many pedals, she was afraid to try one of them. Besides that, she was too busy just steering it. Well, of course, he thanked her for being so cool about it and proceeded on into Albuquerque. He often wondered what would have happened if someone else had decided to double-park in her path. Oh well. All's well that ends well.

We did learn a lesson, however. On this particular model, when we parked with the engine running, we all decided to use a curb when possible, or at least turn the front wheels to minimize any future accidents from this sort of thing.

THE FRIGHTENED LADY

Three bus loads of athletes were to be taken
from Amarillo to Albuquerque one night, and I
received one of those assignments. All buses stayed
together in case of trouble, and the coaches wanted it
that way. Everything was normal from Amarillo to
Clines Corners where we stopped for a break. The
coffee shop was closed, but restrooms and soft drinks
were available in the 24-hour service station.

A loaded station wagon with out-of-state
plates was in the driveway. A lady was talking to
the attendant and she was crying. Out of curiosity,
I asked the attendant what the trouble was. He told
me that before stopping for gas, a car with four

young men had been following and passing them, intimidating the lady and her teenage son. After pulling into Clines Corners, she was approached by the four men who seemed to be under the influence.

The lady had the attendant call the Highway Patrol. Clines Corners had no telephone at that time, only radio communication, and the attendant wasn't able to get through to the police. Hearing the call being made, the men told the lady that they would be waiting down the road and make her regret calling the authorities. So the lady was scared to get back out on the highway.

After hearing her story, I checked with the other two drivers and they agreed she could run with us if she wanted to, as long as she kept up with us. I told the lady that we had three bus loads of male athletes and she was welcome to go to Albuquerque with us. She seemed so relieved, and since she had a new station wagon, she wouldn't have any trouble staying up with us. Albuquerque was only about an hour away.

Telling her to fall in behind the lead bus, I said I was number two and would keep an eye on her. We reminded her that in about thirty minutes we would be going into the mountains, but not to be afraid. The first driver would not lead her into a curve in an unsafe manner, and all she needed to do was stay with the first bus and be assured that those four drunks were not going to bother her. We instructed her to follow us into the station in Albuquerque, have breakfast, and then we would show her how to get back on Route 66 on her way west. The lady seemed quite relieved, and we pulled out. The trip to Albuquerque went without incident.

After the buses unloaded, we joined her in the coffee shop where she offered to buy our breakfast. This we declined, but we thanked her, anyway. She said that in the mountains, she was driving a lot faster than she would normally have driven. She was getting quite anxious when her son reminded her that "these guys know their business." In fact, the young man seemed to be thrilled to be a part of the convoy. The lady informed us that she wasn't used to driving up to eighty mph in the mountains. After breakfast, we told her how to find the highway she needed and after a hug apiece, she continued on her way.

Several weeks later, each of us received a letter of commendation along with a copy of her letter to the company, thanking us for our concern and help. That gave us a nice feeling.

A SMALL VOICE

It was in the early fifties when the Albuquerque dispatcher called me down to the shop one night to pick up an old Silverside bus to be the second section of the 7:30 p.m. eastbound for Amarillo. After taking the bus to the station and since the first section was filled to capacity, I loaded the remainder of the passengers on and headed east on Central Avenue, which was old Route 66. I had noticed the dark clouds hanging low over the Sandia Mountains and, as it was winter, my fears were correct. We ran into icy roads by the time we got to Clines Corners. By the time we arrived at the Club Cafe in Santa Rosa, the roads were a solid sheet of ice.

The first-section driver left town a couple of minutes before I did, and as I climbed the hill out of Santa Rosa, I noticed the bus disappear into the freezing drizzle. It was then in the wee hours of the night and since the weather was bad, the traffic on the old single-lane highway was very light. The old Route 66 road, at that time, came out of Santa Rosa and proceeded due east over a slight mesa which is still visible to this day. As you leave town on Interstate 40, you'll go east for a few miles and the old road will turn back to the northeast into the small village of Cuervo, which is still there ...only now it's on I-40.

This particular night, as I was approaching a long hill and couldn't see over the crest, a small voice (as I jokingly refer to it) told me to come to a complete stop at the top and take a look. This I did, and as I stepped out of the bus, I found that it was almost impossible to stand on the extremely slippery road. As I was shuffling forward, a male passenger got out and asked if he could come along.

Telling him to be careful, we made it to the crest and couldn't believe what we saw. The bus in front of me had tangled with a car and both vehicles were blocking the entire road. It took us several minutes to get to them, where we found the driver of the bus and several passengers were injured. The first driver was very busy trying to get the situation under control. He told me to pack everyone on my bus and proceed to the hospital in Tucumcari about forty-five minutes away.

34

After I finally got back up the hill and literally slid the bus back down, I managed to get everyone aboard by using the rear door on the disabled bus. The men lifted the women and children onto my bus. After getting everyone aboard and determining that no one seemed to be critically injured, I observed mostly just cuts, scrapes, and cold. The first driver had only a few cuts about his face, so he gave me instructions to stop at the first telephone and notify authorities. I was then to proceed with caution to the hospital in Tucumcari. He reminded me to be sure and get everyone's name and address on the witness slips, which was a strict company policy.

He told me that he and the car passengers would be okay until they could get back into Santa Rosa, which was only about fourteen miles. I proceeded on to Tucumcari, which by that time had gotten daylight (which helped a lot), and left everyone who was injured at the hospital. The remainder of the passengers had a seat and I continued on to the bus station for a much-needed rest stop. We had no restroom on the bus and it had been several hours since leaving Albuquerque, so I gave the passengers a full hour to have breakfast and get cleaned up a little.

Most of this hour I spent talking to the Highway Patrol, the Amarillo dispatcher, and the Albuquerque dispatcher. The biggest problem, however, was with concerned passengers who had numerous questions: their baggage was still on the wrecked bus; how long until it caught up? How late are we going to be in St. Louis? etc. The only relief from this constant deluge was to load up and leave. By mid-morning, as we left Tucumcari, the sun had come out and the roads were dry. We arrived in Amarillo in record time to find clean buses and fresh drivers were waiting.

I felt the passengers were the lucky ones, as I was informed that it would be necessary for me to complete a full, seven-page accident report because the first driver was in the hospital in Santa Rosa. Being already dog-tired, I could hardly see straight by then; but after more coffee, I got though it somehow and got to bed by late afternoon. It had been a twenty-four-hour work day.

The following day, I was told to report to my superintendent in Amarillo. He wanted to hear the complete story in person. It was during this interview that I was informed of some other facts. It seemed the first driver had approached the crest of the hill in a normal fashion only to find the car, which was pulling a trailer, had spun out of control and was taking up the entire roadway. The driver had no choice but to ram them. The car's occupants had evidently vacated the vehicle as the bus approached thus preventing more injuries and possible deaths.

The first driver was back to work in a few days and the first thing he asked me was why I had stopped at the top of the hill. Frankly, I told him, I didn't know. The driver then told me that even before he hit the car, he was very concerned about me plowing into his bus. After the crash, when he saw me standing there, he was very relieved.

This is just one more true account of some unexplainable thing that tells us humans what to do. I'll bet everyone who reads this can think of similar experiences that they themselves have had.

Thank you, "Little Voice."

HE LOVES CIGARS

One winter afternoon in Amarillo, as I was checking tickets and loading passengers on a westbound schedule, I noticed an elderly couple standing in line. The man had a cigar in his mouth. The reason that I noticed him was, in those days, the law would allow cigarette smoking on buses, but no cigar or pipe smoking was allowed. By the time the couple got to the door of the bus, I noticed he had put the cigar out, thus relieving me of the necessity of mentioning it to him. I'd rather wait until I made my announcement, which includes the smoking laws, and that was usually sufficient.

The old couple sat on the right front seat, and after loading we pulled out of the station and onto Route 66 heading west. Taking the mike and asking for their attention, telling them about arrival times, rest stops, and a few safety tips, I then made it very clear about the smoking regulations...I thought. Settling down for our two-hour drive to Tucumcari, where we had a short stop before our evening meal stop at Santa Rosa, I had just passed the small village of Newkirk when the smell of a cigar almost knocked me out of my seat. The old gentleman had fired up a big stogie; in fact, it was as long as any I had ever seen.

As he was sitting next to the aisle, I could almost reach out and touch him, so I didn't need to use the PA system. I asked him to please refrain from smoking the cigar until we reached Santa Rosa. The old man might have been hard of hearing and didn't understand, but the lady wasn't--for I remembered her asking me some questions; so I actually turned in my seat and pointed at the man's face and asked again. This time the lady answered me. She said, "Sir, he heard you, but he loves cigars." At this point, I almost stopped the bus, but decided against such drastic action. Even though this was against federal regulations, neither the law nor the company would give us the permission to put anyone off for violating it. Poor me. What could I do at this point?

While this was taking place, we were only a few minutes from Santa Rosa and then all through dinner at the Club Cafe, I kept asking myself what I was to do. It seemed the old couple had me on the spot. But, since several women had complained to me about the smoke, I felt it was decision time. After giving a re-board call, I walked to the rear of the bus to count the passengers. When returning to the front, I noticed that old gentleman had fired that sucker off again. That did it. Enough was enough. I had to get the majority of the people on my side and now was the time to put my plan into action.

Taking my work gloves out of my little bag, I put on my cap and stepped to the outside of the bus for a moment. I then opened the passenger door and flipped a small chrome lever allowing the front section of the passenger door to open about two inches. It was equipped with a big screen and this would allow plenty of air to enter the right side of the bus, right into the old couple's faces. Then as I sat down in the driver's seat, I slipped the one on the left side of the bus and I realized that some of us was afixin' to get a mite cold. It was a bitter cold night outside, but with no rain or snow, and I thought this was the only way; after all, I couldn't break the rules of the company or the law.

As we started out of Santa Rosa en route to Albuquerque, I picked up the mike and explained that, "For a while, you people might get a little cold, but I have no choice. It's 118 miles to Albuquerque and cigar smoke has a way of putting me to sleep." As I was speaking, I glanced up into the passenger mirror and noticed that several people were getting their coats down and smiling. I think they understood what I was doing and agreed with my actions.

41

When I reached about fifty mph, the old lady was yelling at me to close the windows and I didn't answer her the first time around, but kept building up speed. By the time we reached seventy mph, the wind was literally screaming in the side windows. The old lady yelled at me again to close some windows. Looking over at the lady, I told her, "No, after all, I need fresh air; but I would consider it if your husband would reconsider smoking that cotton pickin' cigar." No need to explain further. The old man could hear, after all. He got up from his seat and stomped the cigar out in the step-well, giving me a good, old-fashioned go-to-hell look, and sat back down. I then pulled to the side of the road, opened the passenger door and kicked the cigar-butt out, giving him a small, go-to-hell look. I closed the window, removed my jacket, hat and gloves, and started driving off amidst a round of applause. Turning the heaters up a touch or two allowed everyone to settle down to a pleasant trip.

About an hour and a half later, we arrived in Moriarty about ten minutes ahead of time, and as I was bumping my tires, I decided to try something on the old man. Stepping up into the bus, I motioned for him to lean forward. I then asked him if he would like to step outside and have a smoke with me for a few minutes. The old man grabbed his coat and out he came. We went inside the old service station and smoked together. I asked him where he was from and he turned out to be a very nice person. In fact, he seemed quite thrilled that he was invited out to smoke.

Upon their departure from the bus in Albuquerque, they even told me they enjoyed the trip. They were a little stubborn, but nice. I couldn't help but ponder the question, "Aren't we all?"

THE CHRISTMAS TREE

Leaving Oklahoma City en route to Amarillo while following an Oklahoma City driver on what we jokingly called the "hoot owl" run, I remembered that the only bus stations between there and Amarillo were Clinton and Shamrock. We had quite a few bundles of newspapers to unload, plus it was only about a week before Christmas and both of us were loaded to capacity. Almost every town decorates for Christmas in their own way--some with lights across the streets and all sorts of things. Sayre is an old town with pipe installed in the sidewalks every few feet for the purpose of holding flags, but this year the townspeople decided to put Christmas trees there, instead. They were all about six feet tall with no decorations. As we were unloading papers, I mentioned to the driver that I needed to go shopping for a tree the next day with my wife, as we were late this year in getting one.

I went to the rear of the bus to check the tires and engine and we pulled out for Amarillo. After unloading the passengers at the terminal in Amarillo, we proceeded to the shop to get the bus serviced. This would end our assignment, and as I was gathering up my log book, flashlight, and a few other things, this driver came to the door of my bus holding a six-foot Christmas tree. He told me that after I had turned by back in Sayre, this Christmas tree fell out of its mounting and onto his bus without his knowledge. He didn't know it himself until the baggage man asked him about it.

He told the baggage man that I had purchased it back down the road. This particular driver was always pulling some sorta' prank on people and was a real kick in the pants to work with, but I couldn't help but wonder what some checker's report would have sounded like had one been aboard and witnessed that little event.

Well, it turned out to be a nice Christmas, and we enjoyed the tree. I couldn't help but feel a little guilty, even though I couldn't help it that the little ole' tree had fallen into that bus and I sure couldn't help it that this guy was a real prankster. I'll bet he couldn't help it either, so I decided to enjoy.

Thanks Sayre, and Merry Christmas.

SNOWED-IN AWAY FROM HOME

One January in the late 1950s, I was working the Amarillo extra board, and as usual--when the weather gets bad--it seems that some of the regular drivers like to lay off. The dispatcher called and informed me one afternoon that I would probably go to Albuquerque later that day because one of the older drivers had laid off. Since my wife hadn't been with me on a trip in a long time, she decided to go along. The trip from Amarillo to Albuquerque was fairly routine, but most drivers had a kind of superstition about wives going with their husbands. In fact, some wives refused to go because something unusual would invariably happen. The rest of this story will certainly bear that out.

After arriving in Albuquerque that night, as we walked the short distance to the El Fidel Hotel, we commented on how cloudy and cold the weather had become and jokingly wondered if maybe it might snow. We laughed because snow of any great depth is very rare here in the Rio Grande Valley. The next morning when I woke up, out of habit I guess, I peeked out the window and was very surprised to see three to four inches of snow on the ground and it was still snowing heavily. My wife commented, "Sure. I knew something like this would happen if I came along."

We got dressed and started for the cafe for breakfast, a distance of one block. As we stepped out of the elevator, we ran into an old friend of mine from Amarillo, too. His name was Jack Blanchard, and he had arrived after us, so we all decided to have breakfast together. It was around 9:00 a.m. and I was due out for Amarillo at 12:30 p.m. As we left, my wife was having a hard time getting through the snow in her dress shoes, so we crossed the street and entered a large department store called Fedway to get her some kind of footwear.

We returned to the hotel and while we were sitting in the lobby with several friends, the dispatcher called to tell me that I wouldn't be leaving at 12:30 as the highway had been closed on the eastern side of Albuquerque at the mouth of Tijeras Canyon. He told me to relax, go to a movie, or whatever, because the patrol assured him that the road through the mountains on Route 66 would not be passable until the next morning. All the drivers were used to this sort of thing, but it was getting to my wife.

Other drivers would arrive occasionally from the west as the road was open from Flagstaff, but still closed on east. They advised us that the bus station was getting very crowded and more buses were on the way in. This is very bad, especially for young mothers with children since there were no rooms available in the hotels and motels. In fact, the newscast reported the traffic on Route 66 eastbound was backed-up over ten miles.

That afternoon, out of sheer boredom, we walked every aisle in the Fedway Department Store, looking at everything from guns to girdles and didn't buy a thing. The store personnel didn't seem to mind because, by then, the snow was much deeper and there were no customers anyway. That night, before going to bed, I called the dispatcher and was told to relax 'til morning and maybe something would break.

At about 6:00 o'clock the next morning, the dispatcher called and told me to get breakfast and then show up at the station because the highway patrol had indicated that they might allow some buses around the road block after sunup. By the time my wife and I had eaten and arrived at the station, we couldn't believe the number of people there. The large covered driveway, normally used for bus loading and unloading was jammed with people. We found it very difficult to get inside to the dispatch office.

After squeezing through the people to the dispatch office, I was told to go to the shop and get a double-decked Scenicruiser that had arrived the day before from Flagstaff and to come on up to the station, load to full capacity, and the highway patrol would allow me to go around the road block. The dispatcher told me to leave Route 66 at Moriarty, go south to Encino and Willard, then take Highway 60 east to Clovis and then on to Amarillo. The detour would add about 100 miles to my day's work.

After loading the passengers aboard, we left the station about 8:00 a.m. and pulled onto the highway, which was filled with traffic. They told me to use the incoming lane and by-pass the long line of traffic. After about 12 miles, I arrived at the roadblock and was told by the officer to watch for snowplows and that I shouldn't have any traffic to deal with. He said, "You're on your own. Good luck!" Continuing on up the canyon and finding the traction was very good in the deep snow, I also found visibility was poor, but we kept on rolling right along. Realizing that Sedillo Hill would be coming up soon, I felt that if I could make a good run to start with, I might make it to the summit before spinning out. Having a full load of passengers and baggage was helpful, making the rear of the bus heavier and we finally made it to the summit. The next few miles to Moriarty were down hill and, even though the snow slowed us down, it was no problem.

After turning south at Moriarty and leaving Route 66, I noticed that a rancher or two had made a track in the snow, making it somewhat easier to follow the road. Turning east on Highway 60, we progressed on to the small railroad town of Vaughn, where I parked almost in the middle of the street, and we had our lunch break. There was no traffic to contend with there. After lunch, we continued on east to Clovis. If you've ever been across this part of New Mexico, you know how desolate and lonely it can be. I was moving along fairly steadily, snow was still falling, and by now the passengers were mostly asleep, as they had been through a lot the past night.

We moved along very well to Ft. Sumner, past the large road sign advertising the "Gravesite of Billy the Kid" and on to Clovis then to Hereford. At that time the wind was picking up considerably out of the north and started blowing snow across the road. Drifting was now getting worse. The only thing that was better was that there had been more traffic during the day and the deep ruts were easy to follow.

By now, we were within forty-five miles of my home base of Amarillo, but the darkness was making it worse. It was about here that I noticed a bus identical to the one we were in, sitting on the side of the road, but up on a cement culvert. The bus was empty, so we continued on and about two miles later, there was another Scenicruiser which had run into a tree and the front windshield was broken. This all had a way of telling me to slow down and try to stay on the road. It seemed it took a couple of hours to make the 45 miles on to Amarillo, but we made it without any problems.

Feeling very lucky and very tired, I went into the terminal in Amarillo. The dispatcher informed me that the two buses on the road had attempted the detour to get to Albuquerque earlier that day, but at that time the road conditions were freezing rain and high winds, which actually blew them off the road. I felt even luckier to have had the snow instead of the ice.

As we arrived at our home, my wife pulled off her boots and said to me, "No more, buster, never again and I mean it!"

After quite some time, she did try it again, though.

THE BUS THAT WOULDN'T DIE

In 1954, we received our first multilevel buses called Scenicruisers. They had ten seats on the lower level, plus the restroom, and thirty-three seats on the upper level. The power for these buses was two six-cylinder diesel engines located in the rear of the bus. They drove a semi-automatic transmission, or torque converter, and it seemed that everything had to depend on air pressure to operate properly. If the air pressure fell below a certain point, several systems were inoperable. You couldn't even shift gears if air pressure was too low. Since the bus had two engines, it also had two exhaust pipes under the rear bumper.

Late one afternoon, a driver was approaching Oklahoma City from the west, when the air pressure warning buzzer came on, warning him of a malfunction. Since the buses were new, they had several bugs to be worked out. The driver, instead of stopping the bus as soon as the buzzer came on, decided to try to make it a few more blocks to the station. He didn't realize how much trouble he was getting into. Just as he crossed the intersection, before turning into the station, he found he had no brakes. He tried to shift into neutral, but the clutch was also air-operated and he found that he could not take it out of gear.

The driver told us later that the only thing that worked was the electric horn, so he circled the bus station, blowing his horn for attention. The dispatcher ran along side and yelled for him to hit the emergency stop switches. The driver advised him that he had already tried that, and the bus refused to stop. Someone, seeing what was taking place, called the shop and was told by the mechanic that the emergency stop switch was designed to cut off the air to the engine, causing it to stop running. He was told that one of the engines would not stop running, and the mechanic replied that he would have to call his boss real fast and see if he knew anything else to do.

Meanwhile, the dispatcher, several drivers, and the police were stationed around the bus station keeping everything cleared so he could keep circling safely. The mechanic called back a couple of minutes later and told the dispatcher that the one engine still running was getting just enough air through the exhaust pipe of the dead engine to keep it idling. He told the dispatcher to try sticking a rag into the dead engine's exhaust pipe. But, after about three times around the station, this proved to be unsuccessful, also.

About that time, someone decided that, since the drive train was equipped with a fluid coupling, perhaps the driver could ram into a large pipe retaining fence located at the rear of the station. It was thought the bus would not have enough power to do much damage. This idea was quickly followed, as everyone was tired of trying to stuff a rag up the rear end of this bus while it was still moving. The pipes the bus rammed into were about eight inches in diameter and set in concrete. The driver picked two that the bumper would fit and ram them he did! He said the stop was kinda' sudden and while it stopped the bus, it didn't stop the engine. It continued to run as it sat there bucking and smoking. The passengers were unloaded as quickly as possible and escorted into the station.

By this time, the shop mechanic had arrived and opened up the engine compartment and disconnected the fuel line. After a few more bucks and snorts, the old girl finally died. After this ordeal, several of us had greasy hands from trying to do something to help, and after we all got in the drivers' room to wash up, I've never heard so much laughing in all my life. Many times, I've wished I'd had a tape recording of that.

The driver commented that it was so embarrassing to him, circling the station twelve or thirteen times, especially with all the ribbing he took from the passengers. He said that they were yelling at him, mostly in fun of course, for he was an older driver. Such remarks as, "Did you only start today, driver? Driver, `could I please get off now...if you don't mind!" One fellow said he saw his wife wave to them when they arrived, but after about the tenth time around, he saw her leaving with another man. Another passenger asked him if this was what these new Scenicruisers were supposed to do. A lady asked him if all the stations between there and Chicago had to be circled thirteen times, would they be able to make it this year?

The driver said that sitting there circling with those buzzers sounding off made him kinda' red-faced. As everyone was about to regain their composure, the old dispatcher started in. He pointed to the driver and said, "You? What about me? I'm the professional man around here, the only one with a tie on, and I'm chasing that booger around the station trying to stuff this red rag up its rear end!" Well, that started the laughing all over again. I've never laughed so hard...my sides were really killing me by that time. I'm sure there was some exaggerating going on, but it only added to the humor. One driver said he noticed a wino out by the dumpster, and after about the tenth trip around, he poured his wine out on the ground and walked off.

We noticed that in the months ahead, changes in the systems started coming fairly rapidly and safety features were re-designed from top to bottom. Greyhound's new Scenicruiser didn't make much of an impression on people around there that afternoon, except maybe for the drunk who swore off wine and, of course, the driver...who said he had to go home and "unwind."

GRANDPA'S BEDTIME

The Greyhound drivers would often sit around the drivers' room discussing the reasons why there seemed to be more problems with elderly people between Oklahoma City and Albuquerque than in practically any other geographic location. About the only logical conclusion we reached was the fact that most old people are destitute, in their minds, at least. It doesn't seem to matter how much money an old person has, most are afraid they will run out before they die. It seems to be their biggest dread, and is understandable since most have little way of earning more.

These old people could board the bus on the east coast and ride to the west coast and vice-versa, non-stop because it's cheaper that way. Add to this the fact that the food in bus stations was about as bad as you can get (especially for the elderly) and that their children seemed very anxious to get them out of their hair; it all added up to real anxiety. Relatives who really cared wouldn't have wanted them to make that long bus trip to start with. Our conclusion took into account the fact that we were about in the center of America, so we had about the same amount of problems going east or west, and by the time they got to us, even prune juice wouldn't work anymore. Trying to use that little restroom in the rear of a bus, with a 318 Detroit diesel engine turning at full rpms right under you while traveling that old concrete slab of Route 66 would give anyone understanding about why these old people get confused. The little closet bounced like it was registering about a 9.6 on the Richter scale and I'm sure their bottoms didn't hit the seat a third of the time, much less allow them the desired results.

One evening about sundown heading east to Shamrock for our evening meal stop, I saw an old stately gentleman on the rear seat start taking off his clothes. Stopping the bus and going back to talk with him, I found out he was preparing for his bath and to retire for the evening. He asked me if the bath water was ready. Poor thing. He thought he was home. Several men passengers helped by restraining him and making sure he remained seated for another twenty or thirty minutes. Upon arrival in Shamrock, he was taken to the hospital, and I was told that the next day, after a good night's sleep and some good food, a bath and a seat that didn't buck, he was fine and continued on his way.

Those restrooms were okay for a high school football team of tough athletes, but surely were not designed for the elderly. Maybe that's why they invented airplanes.

A MATTER OF INTERPRETATION

Late one night, I loaded my bus for Albuquerque and all points west of Amarillo. It was a little after midnight, and about the time we cleared the city limits, I fired off a cigarette, opened my little side window, leaned back and got all settled down for the trip to our first rest stop in Tucumcari. I noted that most of the passengers appeared to be asleep. At that time, the laws were very lax concerning smoking on buses. In fact, most of the drivers smoked while driving. There were no restrictions at all about smoking cigarettes; only pipes and cigars were discouraged, and I had heard very few facts or comments about the hazards of smoking at all.

About the time I took my second puff, a little lady on the right front seat said to me, "Driver, I don't think you should smoke them old cigarettes." Asking her, "Why not?", I noticed she had a Bible, trimmed in lace in her lap. When she had entered the bus, I had noticed she was dressed very plain, no makeup or frills of any kind, and she wore small granny-type glasses--the kind that most people look over when talking to someone. She informed me that the cigarettes were bad for me and her and everyone on board. I thought to myself, "Of course, if I go to sleep at the wheel and roll this big double-decker a couple of times, it's gonna' be worse than that for our health!" But to keep the conversation friendly, I informed her that I thought it would be okay because it was in the Bible.

She immediately leaned forward, looking over her metal glasses and informed me that she had read the Bible through several times and smoking was certainly not condoned by any of the holy writers. By then, I noticed the passengers were coming alive, as if they were waiting for the outcome of this little duel--or maybe hoping she would throw the big Bible at me just to have a little action. By this time, I had flipped the butt out the little side window and, still trying to get her to lighten up, I asked her to look in Genesis 24:61 where it said Rebecca and her maids had a pack of camels.

If I'd known so many passengers were awake, I wouldn't have told her that, but it seemed that everyone on the bus was awake and had a big laugh over it. This sort of embarrassed me, for it was not my intention to put her in an embarrassing situation. Too late, I was thinking about how to apologize to her. About that time, the laughter had stopped and she leaned forward and kindly informed me that certainly was not the scriptural meaning of Rebecca's camels. As she was very explicit and sincere, the passengers were again very amused. It made me wonder how all this would appear in case I had one of those hard-nosed checkers aboard.

Oh, well, if the boss calls me in, I thought, I could just quote him the same thing. 'Course, I knew for sure he didn't know anything about the Bible, which brings up this suggestion: anytime any of you have a problem with anyone, in order to make your point, just tell them it's in Ecclesiastes, or something. What the heck, most people don't know the difference, anyway.

SNOW STORM ON ADRIAN HILL

One winter day in the lobby of the Hilton Hotel in Albuquerque, I was trying to find something to do to keep from going bonkers. Having coffee and talking with other drivers and some railroaders who worked for Santa Fe had gotten old. The day before, I had brought over an extra assignment from Amarillo, and was waiting for an assignment back; but due to the lack of business in winter, the job of working the extra board could be quite a waiting game.

About five o'clock that evening, the Albuquerque dispatcher called me to deadhead on the cushions at 7:30 p.m. back to Amarillo. This was quite common for the company to do. It was cheaper for them to pay us half-rate to ride home than to keep paying us lay-over time. Everything went fine, even though the weather had turned a little threatening. When we left Tucumcari, it started to rain and snow, making the trip more difficult. We were still fairly well on time until we came to Glen Rio, which was a small village on the Texas-New Mexico state line. By then, the snow was getting heavier and by the time we had gone a few more miles into Texas, the snow was about five inches deep. Carl commented about the conditions of "Adrian Hill." This was the place where the highway climbs out of the rolling ranch land up the flatland of West Texas, known to all the natives as the "Caprock."

When we approached this long hill, Carl's concerns were justified. We noticed the traffic had stalled and we had to stop also. We could see tail lights of different vehicles all the way to the top and no one seemed to be moving at all. After putting on our raincoats, we left the bus and walked up to the trouble spot to see if we could help. It was about a half mile up where a truck had been doing okay until he came upon a stalled car. The trucker had jack-knifed the truck to avoid a collision.

There were about ten or twelve truckers and motorists shoveling snow from around the rig, and some were bringing sand and spreading it by hand. In these cases, it is common courtesy to help if you can, to get the first one in line out of the way, the second and so on--until your turn comes around.

Invariably, some selfish motorists will let everyone else do the shoveling, then they will dart in and take off ahead of all the rest. This isn't the best course of action around a bunch of tired truckers, as I will explain.

The men had already gotten several motorists free and over the hill. Now it was time to see if the old Peterbilt could get out. We had all backed up out of the way, while the truck driver was getting ready to give it a try. We had removed all the snow from in front of the truck and sanded a path for the drive wheels. It was then we noticed a car approaching from down the hill, coming around all the other vehicles and trying to get to the top. It turned out to be a young couple in a VW beetle. The little car got within about fifty yards of us, when one of the truckers yelled at his buddies and they lined up-- shovels in hand--causing the young man to stop.

He rolled down his window and one of the truckers asked him, "Just where the hell do you think you're going?" The young man told him to Ohio and the truck driver informed him that he would not be allowed to go ahead of everyone else, but he would be given a shovel, if he wanted to help. The young man gave the car the gas and tried to make a run for it. The truckers then surrounded the little car and shoved it backwards into a deep snow-drift. The trucker told the man, "Now you'll just sit there out of the way until everyone else gets out. Then maybe you can figure a way out on your own."

By now, the trucker had put the Peterbilt in gear and the drive-wheels began to grab and take hold. He applied no acceleration to the engine, just left it idling so as not to spin. The cab started jumping up and down as the eight wheels on the tractor started to grab. Both of his axles were of the anti-lock variety and he said they wouldn't spin a lot. He was right. As the powerful Cummins engine sat idling, the rig began to inch forward amidst cheers from everyone. The trucker eased the big rig up onto the roadway, and as he topped the hill, he shifted to another gear, blinked his lights a couple of times, blew his airhorn to say thanks, and that was the last we saw of him.

After the truck was gone, the other vehicles began to move out in an orderly fashion. By the time we walked back to the bus, we had but a few minutes to wait, then we also joined the convoy and proceeded on to Amarillo.

The plight of the young couple in the VW is not known. At least they were young, and could figure out a way to keep warm! It reminded me of the statement someone made: "It's hell growin' up!"

THE POST OFFICE ROBBER

As I had been working for several years and building up experience, I was asked to do some relief dispatching--calling drivers when needed, sending and receiving teletypes, etc. The dispatch office was located across and to the rear of the terminal with a good view of the driveway. It was a wintry day and the weather was fairly cold when a couple of nicely-dressed gentlemen came into my office and identified themselves as FBI agents. They told me they were looking for a post office robber from Arkansas and they would be inspecting the passengers as they departed the buses.

The men left the office and for the next couple of days, we didn't even know where they were. They were very inconspicuous. I think it was the third night when they re-appeared to inform me they were leaving since they suspected the wanted man had not chosen to come through Amarillo. A couple of hours later, a city police unit came into the driveway, parked in front of the dispatch office, informed me they were there to apprehend a post office robber from Arkansas, and they would be inspecting incoming passengers arriving from the east.

As they sat in my office talking about how this fellow should be taught a lesson for coming through Amarillo, the talk became rough and mean. They said the suspect was rather tall, probably carrying an overcoat on his arm, probably armed and dangerous. A few minutes before a schedule was due in from the east, the cigar-chewing officer told his partner to get the shotgun from the car.

After asking them if they planned to leave the police unit in plain sight, and if a shotgun might be used in the midst of passengers, I was informed that they were in charge of this operation. In a few minutes, a bus arrived and these two officers stood close to the door of the bus as the passengers started filing off. When a tall, lean man, wearing a cowboy hat and carrying a coat started to get off, the officers nabbed him and escorted him back to the dispatch office for questioning.

It turned out that the suspect was a sheriff's deputy from Oklahoma on his way to Tucumcari, to pick up a prisoner. As the red-faced officers tried to explain to the deputy, I could see the difference in the procedure of the well-trained FBI personnel and the local police.

As they were getting into their unit to leave, I couldn't resist telling them, "Y'all come back now, ya' hear?"

A COUPLE OF BEERS

En route from Amarillo to Oklahoma City, the bars were just closing when I was leaving El Reno with about twenty passengers on board. The trip over old Route 66 had been fairly routine and now the road into Oklahoma City was a four-lane highway. Noticing a car following me, I watched carefully for it might be a late passenger, the police looking for someone, or just kids, with nothing better to do, planning to race the old bus, thinking it was loaded with pretty girls.

But it was a drunk driver, and he was gaining on me. Pulling out to pass, he moved up even with the front of the bus. Suddenly he pulled to the right so fast that I had no time to respond. The next few seconds seemed like a year. The rear door of his old clunker came in contact with my front bumper, scooting him down the road sideways. The side of his car rose up in front of me with lots of glass breaking. His old tires blowing out sounded kinda' like firecrackers.

As I was standing on the brakes, trying to stop, I was wondering, "Lord, how many people are in that thing?" I could imagine a whole family being killed right in front of my eyes and I was virtually helpless. But, as I was finally getting stopped, it seemed that the old bus had enough of that crap and pushed the old clunker off into the ditch on the right side. I was stopped before the car hit the right bank, but the car had stirred up so much dirt, that I couldn't see a thing.

When the dust cleared, I noticed the car was laying on its left side, with the right side shaped somewhat like a half-moon. Turning on my flashers, I grabbed a flare and my flashlight, set off the flare, and arrived at the car just as this fellow was crawling out of one of the windows that was now gone. By then, a couple of male passengers came out and helped me get him out the rest of the way. He didn't seem hurt, not even a scratch. After inspecting the interior of the car, I found he was the sole occupant. Boy, was that a relief!

As we climbed back down off the old car, the driver yelled, "Just what the hell do you mean trying to run over a feller like that?" Since there were no apparent injuries, I started laughing and he said,

"Well, I don't think it's a laughing matter fer damn sure."

The police came almost immediately. Someone had probably seen the accident and called them. It didn't take long for them to get the drunk in their gentle care. After observing all the skid marks, they found that he had definitely pulled into me. When I checked the passengers, I found that most of them were still asleep and had to tell them about the accident. Most of them just thought I had stopped for some reason. The bus had no damage, only a scratch or two on the front bumper and I didn't even lose a headlight.

While sitting in the police car making reports, and exchanging names and addresses, etc., one of the officers asked the fellow how much he had been drinking. He answered, "I only had a couple of beers." The officer looked at me and remarked that he hoped, before he retired, he would pick up just one drunk that would admit to having three. He told the driver that you don't shove Greyhound buses around with just two beers.

HIGHWAY FATALITIES

One afternoon in Oklahoma City, I was given an assignment about 4:00 p.m. to take an empty bus to Amarillo. This was a common practice in order to keep the equipment properly distributed. Assigned to follow the regularly scheduled bus due out at 5:00 p.m., I parked waiting for the other driver to load. We signed out together, and I was to follow him to Amarillo and be available, if needed.

We made all the necessary stops along Route 66 arriving in Shamrock about 9:50 p.m. and after a fifteen-minute rest stop, we left Shamrock to drive a newer version of Route 66. It was four lanes for a short distance, not the interstate, only a four-lane with crossings occasionally.

The bus I was following was a double-decked Scenicruiser and the one I was driving was a regular single-level bus. We were always instructed to follow at least a quarter mile apart. I remember watching the tail lights of the front bus pass through a small village called Lela, located six miles west of Shamrock. At that time, I noted the time was 10:20 p.m. Little did I know, at that moment, and for the next twenty-four hours, life would be pure chaos for me and three people were only seconds away from sudden death. Following are some of the things I will remember the rest of my life.

Approaching Lela from the east at about fifty-five mph in the far right-hand lane, I did not know that three people were also approaching the intersection at about sixty-five mph. The speed of the car, plus some other facts that were told to me later by the law officers and eventually facts and rumors from truckers and witnesses all contributed to the final outcome. As you will see, I was too busy for quite some time to know what happened without being told.

As I approached the village, I glanced over to my left, which was the only road entering the highway, and my attention was captured by headlights on the high beam approaching at a high rate of speed. Realizing the vehicle could not possibly come to a stop at the stop sign, I then moved to the right and applied the brakes to the maximum. The bus's right front wheel had entered the sand at the side of the road and all four wheels were beginning to leave skid marks. The next thing I recall was a fairly good jolt, which at the point of impact swayed the bus to my left, then when the bus came back upright, the momentum took it right and into an old wrecking yard located just off the shoulder of the road.

At this point, it was terribly quiet, the bus engine had quit running, too, and the front passenger door was jammed. I grabbed my flashlight and a couple of flares and jumped out of the rear door (on this particular model, emergency doors were required). I didn't even think about myself being hurt, but had to find out what was going on outside. As I got out of the bus and started looking around with my flashlight, all I could find were pieces of glass and assorted junk. I kept calling out, "Is there anyone out there? Where are you? Can you hear me?"

There was only silence, and I couldn't even find the vehicle that had hit me. Then I heard a car approaching from the east, so I started flagging with my flashlight. It turned out to be a teenager and his girlfriend. I asked him to return to Shamrock and to notify authorities of a very bad accident. He obligingly left immediately.

Looking west about half a mile, I could see the marker lights of a big rig coming up over the hill at a very high rate of speed. I fired off a flare and threw it as high as I could in the direction of the east-bound lanes. Later, I found out this was a Trans-Con driver who lived in Oklahoma City. As soon as he saw the flare, he started coming to a stop, realizing an accident was probably ahead. He said the flare saved him from plowing into the wrecked vehicle, which had wound up in the center of his lane of traffic.

After throwing the first flare, I then threw another one back behind the bus in the center of the road. The truckers were very helpful in securing the area with more flares and flashing lights. A driver came to me, took hold of my arm and started showing me some bodies; using his flashlight, we located two women and one man.

Two DPS officers arrived on the scene, along with an ambulance. As I sat in a patrol unit, I answered questions from the officers as they were making out their reports. The ambulance had reached the hospital and the report to the officers on their radios was that all three victims were D.O.A. As I was already very nervous, I guess I got the chills. A trucker must have noticed, for he handed me a cup of coffee.

The officers reassured me and told me not to let it get me down. I, apparently, was just an innocent victim of circumstance, and there was nothing I could have done to prevent the mishap. Since the road did not continue beyond the four-lane, they would probably have been killed anyway, and that we should all be thankful the car hit the empty bus instead of a full one or a family in a passenger car. They were very helpful.

I called the dispatcher from a lady's house nearby to report the accident. That call started quite a flurry of activity within the Greyhound organization. Our safety expert left Dallas immediately, so I had to wait in the bus station in Shamrock for his arrival. In the meantime, a lady reporter from Shamrock had arrived out at Lela and called the story into the Amarillo Globe News. The dispatcher in Amarillo had called my wife and told her that I had been in an accident, but had not been injured.

The DPS officer had noticed my left shirt arm was torn at the elbow and had one of the medics look at it. It was slightly scratched, so he put a Band-Aid on it. This led the papers to report that the driver had been injured. Oh, well. Everything was total confusion then, anyway.

The bus I had been following had gone over the hill just west and around a curve when the accident happened, so the driver didn't know what had happened to me. He thought I would be along any minute. When he arrived in Amarillo at 12:30 a.m., he asked the dispatcher if he had heard from me. The dispatcher handed him the midnight edition of the paper and let him read all about it. The reporter from Shamrock had called the story in just before the paper went to press.

The safety officials and big-wigs from Greyhound started arriving about sunrise to start their investigation. We went out to the scene and could tell a lot more in daylight than we could in the dark. The safety man noticed the 1957 Chevrolet had impacted the bus at the front wheel, and then, after discharging its occupants, was hurled 250 feet back across the east-bound lanes. He also reminded me that, had I been in a car, the impact would have been at the driver's door. He showed me the skid marks of the bus, showing the right front wheel was digging into the sand when the car hit. The skid marks continued on after impact, but the car had only moved the bus over one inch. The bus then plowed into several wrecked cars at the salvage yard that had no fence around it.

Evidently, the car came through the stop sign, crossing both east-bound lanes, the median, and about three-fourths of the west-bound lanes before impact. The car left no skid marks.

Anytime a fatality occurs involving a bus, the driver is automatically out of service until the investigation has been completed. Later that afternoon, my supervisor from Amarillo informed me that I could finally go home, but on the way, we would go by the Amarillo air terminal to pick up our claims officer, who was coming in from Dallas. Being worn out, I waited in the car and it wasn't long before the man appeared. The first thing this fellow from Dallas said to me, after shaking my hand, was, "Howard, I hope, for your sake, that you obtained witness slips from the people involved." Being somewhat stunned by this, I was staring at the stupid jerk when the Amarillo supervisor told him that since I was the only survivor, there were no other witnesses. He did have the grace to seem slightly embarrassed.

After arriving home, I fell into bed, exhausted from being up about thirty-six hours. We received quite a few calls from friends and relatives because the papers stated that I was injured, which, of course, was false. After several days, the company concluded that the accident was unpreventable, with no fault on my part and put me back to work with no loss of pay. I never knew their names, but my thanks went out to all who were so helpful--the dating teenagers, the DPS officers, the truckers, and everyone else involved who were so very supportive.

To this day, as I pass through Lela, I can't help but wonder why those people disregarded the stop sign on a major highway. I have been asked by many if liquor was involved. I don't know, as the company was very secretive about the blood-test results. Whatever litigation was entered, I, the driver, was kept in the dark.

One thing for certain, life is very fragile and can come to an end so very fast. Drive carefully!

THE LADIES' LOUNGE

I was called to work one winter morning back in the early fifties in Albuquerque. My assignment was the usual--to take a bus back to my home base in Amarillo. Arriving at the shop, which was only a few short blocks from the El Fidel Hotel, I picked up an old Silverside bus, which was not equipped with a restroom. In fact that model didn't have a PA system or power-steering, but was considered very trustworthy and usually very good in snow, because it was such a heavy model.

This particular morning was rainy and cloudy, but I didn't think anything about it. After loading the passengers, I started out of town. The farther I traveled up Central Avenue toward the mountains, the more snow flakes mixed with rain began to fall. By the time I got out in Tijeras Canyon, the snow was getting fairly heavy on the road. The traffic was keeping the snow off the surface fairly well, but our speed was reduced quite a bit as old Route 66 was then a single lane. It was impossible to pass anyone until we reached the summit.

By the time I had made the twenty-nine miles to Moriarty, then called Buford, the snow was getting heavier. The people who ran the bus station there had no specific information about the conditions of the old road between there and Santa Rosa, so I continued on for about twenty-five miles and pulled in at Clines Corners for a rest stop. I tried to explain to the passengers it might be a good idea for everyone to take advantage of this opportunity to see to their needs, because in this kind of weather, you can't guarantee just when the next stop might be. This was especially aimed at mothers with small children. I noticed a young woman covered with an expensive-looking coat sleeping and I touched her on the shoulder to wake her up. I asked if she wanted to go inside the restaurant while we had a few minutes, but she replied rather curtly, "No, thank you!"

After re-boarding, we headed east from Clines Corners, but with more difficulty as the snow was getting deeper and deeper. After a few more miles, I noticed the blowers inside the bus that furnished the heat had almost stopped. Even the defrosters had very little air output. Consequently, all the windows were getting icy on the inside. The passengers were covering up with anything they had. Knowing that the generator had gone out, I knew we would need a place to stop fairly soon, but as we had already passed "Flying C" Ranch (which was just another tourist trap), I began to try to think of a place to stop. This part of New Mexico was very sparsely occupied. The only place I could think of was a very small station and saloon (I didn't even know its name) and I couldn't remember whether or not I had already passed it.

Another hill or so on, I spotted the small adobe on my left. There were no signs of life, but I thought I could see smoke coming out a chimney every once in a while (since it was snowing and blowing, I couldn't be certain.) and there were a couple of vehicles in the back, so I decided to give it a try. Pulling up in front, as close to the door as possible, I made my way to the door, which hadn't been used because the snow had drifted quite high. Knocking on the door several times, it was a while before a teenage Mexican girl finally opened it slightly. I think she was surprised to see the bus and I asked her if they were open. Not understanding English, she seemed rather reluctant to answer. The place was dark inside since, I assumed, they had no reason to open in a snowstorm. Finally a Mexican lady came up who could understand English fairly well. After learning of our plight, she invited us inside and she proceeded to turn on the lights and told me she would start some coffee. Man, that sounded good to me.

So, I went back to the bus to tell the people that we would be here until we could get a relief bus and that could be quite a while. The Mexican family went out of their way to make us comfortable by building a nice fire in an old wood stove and making sandwiches and other food available. Using their phone, which surprisingly worked, to report our predicament, I then got a cup of coffee and sat down for a little rest.

Every once in a while, a passenger would go through the kitchen and out the back door, and it didn't take me long to figure out that some had already found the restroom, which was a two-hole outhouse about fifty yards behind the saloon. Using it myself, I could attest to the fact that it "don't take long when it's cold!" It sure reminded me of my boyhood days back in Crosbyton.

After we had been inside for almost an hour, this floozy lady finally woke up and decided that the bus was getting too cold even for her fur coat. Frankly though, I'll admit that I had been so busy that I had forgotten all about her. After entering, she stopped and looked all around, clutching the fur coat tightly around her neck. She was probably looking for the 'ladies' sign, which didn't exist. She then walked over to the counter where the teenager was standing and asked the girl something. The girl, not understanding, asked her to repeat the question. The lady, by then very annoyed at the situation, leaned over very close to the girl and asked very loudly, "The lounge, the lounge, the ladies' lounge, where is it? Where is it?"

The girl, by then, had started looking for her mother for some help. I decided at this time to take over since I had brought the lady in here, so I walked up behind the lady and tapped her on the shoulder. As she looked at me, I told her that this was not Grand Central Station, but I would be glad to show her the lounge. Taking her by the arm, I led her through the kitchen and opened the back door, showing her the little wooden 'lounge' sitting all alone out in the snow. Since I had lost my patience with her by this time, I told her to just follow the tracks and she couldn't miss it. In fact, I told her she didn't even have to flush it. She grunted and started down the path, out of necessity, I'm sure. I returned to my coffee amid some clapping of hands from the other passengers, who evidently didn't care for the fancy lady's attitude, either. One grandmotherly-looking woman, who had been helping some of the young mothers, looked over at me with a grin and remarked, "Sir, I hope you enjoyed that as much as we did!" She then thanked me for finding the place and making arrangements for us to stay warm.

All the other passengers were very pleasant and very understanding. The lady had no choice but to return through the kitchen and was asked if she would like to sit and have something to eat. She answered with a definite "No!" and asked me why I hadn't anticipated the bus failure. Then, with a few more slurs, she informed me that she would definitely fly next time, at which point I couldn't restrain myself as I replied to her, "Oh, God, I hope so!"

The other passengers, being fed up with such nonsense, started laughing at her, and again I tried in vain to get her to let up and eat something. She then remarked that she would rather freeze to death and stormed out the front door and returned to the cold bus. We speculated that maybe she was on a liquid diet and perhaps she had her own anti-freeze.

After about another three hours, the relief bus showed up and we all tipped and thanked the Mexican family for their hospitality and continued on to Amarillo where we found the "lounges" marked and very warm.

Throughout the years, I have found that the majority of people are very kind and generous during any kind of hardship.

THE BRITISH SNOW STORM

About 2:30 one hot summer afternoon, while leaving the Albuquerque Hilton Hotel on my way to the bus station, I noticed large thunderheads building on the far side of the Sandia Mountains to the east. I figured this would be a stormy night for me as that was the direction I would be going. I was due out at 3:30 p.m. mountain time and due into Amarillo at midnight central time with a forty-five minute meal stop at the Club Cafe in Santa Rosa and another fifteen-minute stop in Tucumcari. The bus was a through bus from San Francisco to Atlanta. After it was serviced, I loaded the passengers and headed east.

After climbing up out of Albuquerque to the summit of what we called Comers Hill, the clouds were now looking really dark and stormy. Before arriving at Clines Corners, I had noticed the traffic had stopped and the hill up ahead was covered with hail. We were stopped and waited about half an hour before a snow plow arrived and cleared a path for the traffic and we started moving again. The hail had stacked up in places, resembling six-inch deep snow, and an elderly couple from England on the right front seat kept referring to it as snow. Maybe the highway department should have sent a "hail plow." About four miles later, the plow pulled to the side allowing the traffic to pull into Clines Corners, which had a large restaurant.

This storm was tracking east, as most of them do in this part of the country, and it looked as if we were catching up to it. At that point, I had to make a decision whether to go on and take my chances or to stop at Clines Corners and wait it out. We weren't allowed to have CB radios, so I was not in touch with anyone that could give any road information. Thinking the hail could be over, and perhaps had changed to rain (in which case, I would be in front of the storm before long), I decided to go for it. After the traffic pulled off, I was in front, but on my own, as the snow plow had stopped. It wasn't long before I caught up with the storm and it started to rain and the "British" snow was coming down heavily, about the diameter of a quarter. The noise inside the bus was terrible, and the passengers had to shout at one another to be heard.

Thinking, at this point, that I might not have made the right choice, I wondered if my windshield or the one upstairs would be broken. My top speed was only about twenty mph and I knew at this point that I couldn't outrun the storm. Since I-40 had been completed, we would stop under an over-pass and rest for a few minutes before continuing. The quarter-size hail and the rain lasted for about sixty miles and it took over three hours to make that distance. Arriving in Santa Rosa, the Club Cafe was closed. In fact, it looked as if all of Santa Rosa was closed. All the lights were out in town, the heavy rain continued, and I told the passengers to tighten their belts, and I'd try for Tucumcari, about another sixty miles.

Pulling back up on I-40, the traffic seemed to be moving quite fast, which was encouraging, and after only a short time, the rain slacked off slightly and normal highway speed was resumed. Little did I know that one more scary incident was yet to take place.

A few miles east of Santa Rosa, I was coming up on an overpass and I approached a freighter with double trailers which are called "puppies." As I was going faster than the truck, I moved over to the passing lane and started to pass. The mist that the truck was creating cut the visibility, but feeling it was safe to pass, I moved up alongside the truck. Then lightening lit up the countryside and I could suddenly see I-40 was under water about two hundred yards ahead.

Poor me. I never dreamed of such a thing in this dry climate of New Mexico, but there it was. Now what? The truck driver saw the water at about the same time, and I could either slam on the brakes, which would probably cause me to go into a skid possibly into the truck, or go off the road entirely. Either case could be disastrous.

The only other alternative would be to floor-board the bus and hope to outrun the truck into the water and, with full-power, maybe I could make it across ahead of him. Choosing to go, I slammed the accelerator to the floor and plowed into the water at full speed. I had never seen so much brown water in my life. Water went completely over the top of the bus and it seemed like forever before I could see anything. The water slowed the bus down considerably, but we didn't hydroplane out of control and we got through with flying colors.

Checking the right mirror as soon as I could, I still couldn't see the truck because of all the water I had splashed up. The truck made it okay, and he stopped at the bus station, and over coffee, we had a good laugh about the whole thing. He told me that after he realized we were going into the water, he was real thankful that I had the cool head to keep on going. He said he was certain that he couldn't stop either and when he realized I had applied full power, he put power to the tractor and hoped for the best. He, too, was surprised that when the water cleared a little, we had both made it through without incident. I told him that I wasn't trying to be cute by outrunning him, but had no other option. He agreed and seemed proud that we both made the right decision; since by braking, either one of us would probably have gotten someone killed.

After the rest stop in Tucumcari, we continued on to Amarillo on dry road without any more trouble. Even being three hours late didn't keep me from feeling good. Several passengers told me what a good job I had done. Possibly, they were just thankful to be there. I know I was.

The day will long be remembered, according to the British couple.

GUNNIN' FOR ROMEO

About 4:00 o'clock one afternoon, the Oklahoma City dispatcher called me to report for the 5:00 p.m. westbound schedule. After getting ready, I walked the half-block from the Black Hotel to our drivers' room and dispatch office which were next door to the bus station. Just before arriving at the doorway, a man rushed out looking sort of disgruntled. He was wearing coveralls, and looked to be in his mid-thirties. Asking the dispatcher what that was all about, I expected him to tell me the man had lost luggage, a lost ticket, or some of the other many 'normal' complaints. The dispatcher was visibly shaken and replied, "You ain't gonna' believe this, but that fellow walked up to the window and laid a 45 caliber pistol down and demanded to know, 'Where is that S.O.B. that's been sleeping with my wife while I'm working at night?'"

The dispatcher, quite talented in handling normal complaints, said that for a while he was speechless. He finally talked the fellow into putting the gun back in his pocket, and had him explain what this was all about. The man told him that he was looking for the driver who had a small black mustache and wavy dark hair; that he had been seen slipping out of his house early one morning by a neighbor, and his wife had finally broken down and given her husband a fairly good description of the guilty driver. The dispatcher and I knew beyond any doubt who the person was, but that he didn't live in Oklahoma City and didn't drive in and out of there on a regular basis.

I asked the dispatcher if he knew where "Romeo" was, and he stated that he had sent out a teletype and hoped he would get the answer shortly. About that time, the teletype started chattering. The dispatcher looked at it, turned to me wiping his brow and said, "Whew, he's in Albuquerque." At that time, we walked over to the station for some much-needed coffee. As we were sitting there, we tried to think of any other drivers with possible resemblances. Suddenly, the dispatcher said, "Oh my God! It just dawned on me, so and so (he mentioned another driver's name) is en route right now from Amarillo to Oklahoma City and will arrive about 9:00 p.m.!"

This particular driver also had a small, black mustache and dark wavy hair. But this fellow had his home here, was a nice family man and we knew that his appearance was the ONLY similarity with "Romeo." I asked the dispatcher if the avenging husband might go on and forget it. He told me that the man would be standing on the dock observing every driver for the next twenty-four hours if he followed through on this threats. He had also told the dispatcher that it wouldn't do any good to call police, for if they came and searched him, they would not find the gun. The dispatcher figured that the guy probably put the gun in a locker or some hidden place until he was satisfied he had the right man identified.

About that time, I had to load up and head west, but after a day or so, I was back in Oklahoma City and found out the rest of the story. The dispatcher tried several times, after we finished our coffee, to call Clinton before that driver was due out to warn him of the reception party waiting in Oklahoma City. As usual, the line was always busy, as it was only a commissioned agency and therefore had no teletype or company personnel. By the time he finally got the call through, the driver had already left for Oklahoma City.

The dispatcher said that when this particular bus rolled up to the dock, he noticed the fellow in coveralls moving around to a better position. It was always a strict rule that we drivers had to have caps on our heads when loading or unloading passengers, even though we could remove them while driving.

This driver opened the door and stepped out, without his hat, with a crew-cut hair do, and (would you believe?) he didn't even have a mustache, he was clean-shaven. The dispatcher then noticed the would-be-gunman was walking over to another bus that had arrived, completely satisfied that the first driver was not the man. Afterwards, there were a lot of different stories and rumors about what form of communications were used to get the proper results, but no one seemed to know or care about revealing all the facts.

As I recall, this innocent driver wore his hair short for quite a while after that, and also, as the story goes, when "old Romeo" did finally get back to Oklahoma City, he took a cab to the hotel and kept a very low profile. The innocent driver never did tell me how he found out, but we didn't have CB radios or any form of communication, he would only grin and say "E.S.P."

This just proves that you don't have to BE guilty to APPEAR guilty.

THE CHRISTMAS PEANUTS

Several years ago, about ten days before Christmas, I was called to take a second section of a bus schedule to Oklahoma City. After loading my bus, I was on my way across the driveway to the dispatch office to sign out, when I spotted another driver with his hand in a large burlap sack taking out a few peanuts. There was a small hole in the sack about the size of a golf ball. He told me that this one hundred-pound sack of roasted peanuts had just arrived from Portales en route to some eastern destination, but that since it had to change buses in Amarillo, it would probably be delayed, depending on space. He doubted its success for a safe arrival anyway, so we might as well enjoy a few morsels. That's all the encouragement I needed because, as everyone knows around this part of the country, Portales peanuts are the very best. Besides all that, shucks, it was Christmas, wasn't it?

After arriving back in Amarillo the next evening, I couldn't help but notice the sack was still sitting in the same place, but the hole had grown to about the size of a large grapefruit and the contents had gone down considerably. Since the sack was there, and I was there, I was compelled to replenish my supply of the tasty little critters.

Later, after being off for about ten hours and reporting back to the station for another run, I realized passenger traffic was now going at a fairly good pace, so we would not be off for long. While crossing the driveway, I noticed the sack was now only about one-third full, and the entire top of the sack had been ripped open. Again re-stocking my jacket pocket, I told myself, "After all, I might get stuck in a raging blizzard and be without food for days and days." At that point, self-pity took the best of me, so I just loaded up the other jacket pocket. After all, what peanut company in its right mind would want a bus driver to starve to death while fighting a raging blizzard?

About twenty-four hours later, I arrived back in Amarillo. After unloading my passengers, I was kind of surprised to find the remains of the sack and its contents still there. The sack looked as if it had been hit full speed by a king-size Texas tornado...twice...and the only things remaining were a few pieces of yellow webbing and a few peanut hulls. At this point, I couldn't help but be reminded of the many interstate rules and federal regulations concerning shipments. In fact, all drivers had to be bonded and were constantly reminded that stealing anything would be cause for immediate dismissal. Being quite sure that we had no one in this position who would consider stealing anything, I reasoned, "Here it is Christmas time, a sack full of freshly roasted peanuts just standin' out there all alone...who in his right mind could blame any red-blooded American for taking just a sample or two? Stealing' a car or something like that, well that's one thing, but a few peanuts...Bah...it's Christmas."

Surely the claim agent who had to settle with the peanut people wasn't too pleased; in fact, I'll bet he didn't even tell them "Merry Christmas!"

THAT STINKIN' CHRISTMAS

Approaching Christmas holidays one year in the early fifties, the Amarillo Greyhound bus station was becoming very busy, taking in more packages than could be shipped out. People working there began to notice a very obnoxious odor and tried to locate the origin, but to no avail. The odor began to permeate the ticket area and some offices. I'm talkin' an odor that would stink a dog off a gut wagon. The supervisor ordered all packages inspected one by one, but nothing could be found.

The frustrated supervisor, not knowing what to do next, called a friend who worked at a funeral home and asked if he knew of anything that might be sprayed around the place to at least mask the odor. The man came over and sprayed, but it only made the odor smell sweeter. By this time, the employees were beginning to make jokes about it. One guy suggested that maybe someone killed his mother-in-law and cut her up in little pieces in order to get her out of his hair. One fellow even started a story that an old woman was murdered in the same building way back, and this was probably her way of using her spiritual powers to get even. If it wasn't for that dad-blasted stink, it would've been funny.

A couple of nights later, I received an assignment to be the second section to a schedule bound for Albuquerque and I was to double a driver named John Hughes, who happened to be quite a practical joker. We both loaded our buses and pulled out on old Route 66. Our habit was to stop for coffee at a small cafe in Glen Rio on the Texas-New Mexico state line. As John and I were sitting there, he told me that he had been thinking about that smell since leaving Amarillo and was convinced that he knew the answer. He went into a rather lengthy, and I must say, convincing tale about the transplantation of eyeballs. He told me that a clinic in California was shipping them to this place in Boston for research, and that in his opinion, the dry ice had probably been depleted.

This kind of stuff was new to me, so the idea of such a thing was kinda' sickening. I couldn't help but notice that, as we went toward Tucumcari, even the tail lights on cars reminded me of eyeballs and that I was rubbing my eyes quite a bit...as if I was making sure they were still in place.

We had a breakfast stop in Tucumcari, and as I was about to cut up my "over-easy" eggs, ole' John, not willing to let this thing die out, looked over at my eggs and said, "I'll bet that's the way those ole' eyeballs back in Amarillo look about now." At that point, I didn't find those dumb ole' eggs too appealing. To this day, I eat my eggs scrambled.

The next day, as we arrived back in Amarillo, we found the station smelling fairly good. The baggage man told us that they literally tore the baggage room apart and found a box that had fallen behind a counter. It contained a thawed-out turkey some grandmother was shipping to someone.

We all hoped that the lady would learn to ship peppermint. We realized later that, if you want to insult a fellow employee in the baggage room, just call 'em "Turkey!"

BOMBS - A-WA -A -A -A -A ---

DIVE BOMBING

In the early fifties, there were numerous small service stations on old Route 66, many of which were the "mom and pop" variety. This is a story about one of them located a few miles east of Clines Corners. There was a very famous hill, called Palma Hill out there. It was famous not only for the difficulty that a lot of vehicles had getting to the top, but also for the ability to "dive bomb" off the hill in order to build up momentum for climbing the next one. This was especially true for trucks and buses.

At the bottom of this famous hill was a small service station with living quarters in the rear. The couple who lived there, like many others, subscribed to the Albuquerque paper as their only source of daily news. The papers were delivered to the bus station during the night and different buses would take them to the designated locations.

Early one morning, as I was loading the passengers on an eastbound bus, the baggage men placed a fairly large pile of single-rolled papers next to the front wheel. Before leaving the station, I would usually place them in the aisle next to my right foot so I could read the label and "air-mail" them at the proper time. The term "air-mail" was used by the drivers to describe the throwing of the paper.

The older buses had large windows which could be rolled down, allowing us to get a fairly good swing. If the paper was to be delivered to the left side of the road, it was quite simple; but if it was to be delivered on the right side, you had to almost stand up in order to get your left arm out of the window far enough to throw the paper over the top of the bus.

This particular morning, as I started off Palma Hill, I reached down and got the paper and started my "dive-bombing" run. The target was a small sign located about the center of the old gravel driveway. Bus speed was increasing rapidly, window down, paper held firmly in right hand, it was now time. to check for oncoming traffic. If none was approaching, it was much easier as we could go to the far left side of the road to give us a few more feet of delivery advantage.

Since there was no traffic, I started the final maneuver by going to the left side of the highway. The speed of the bus had now reached about eighty mph. With the wind howling past the window, and the bus about one-hundred yards from the driveway, I told myself it was time to "fire." Leaning to the right and with all my might, I let the paper go. I was confident I was going to be successful this time, for I had missed that sign for years. Wrong. That cotton-pickin' paper hit the rear-view mirror. The wind caught those loose papers and blew about half of them back inside the bus.

After managing to get the bus back on the right side of the highway, I heard a lady scream out. I checked the passenger mirror to see several passengers fighting the loose papers and asking each other where they were coming from. Rolling the window back up as I was pulling out of the "dive," so to speak, I couldn't help but feel sorry for the people who were expecting their paper. I would have to sharpen my aim and consider the mirror next time; maybe, I'd hit that sign someday.

Not too long ago, while traveling on I-40, I noticed some old rocks. They're all that's left of the old station. I reflected back in time with the full knowledge that my target was never hit, and couldn't help but wonder how often those folks actually received a readable paper. Maybe they didn't expect to, but found it was worth the price just to witness the "dive-bombing" run.

113

ONE THOUSAND COWS

Old Route 66, leaving Texas into Oklahoma, had a slight "S" curve before coming to a very small village called Texola. Late one rainy night, I was the second section heading for Oklahoma City from Amarillo. Usually, at this time of night, there was nothing open, no traffic, and certainly no activity of any kind, so most of us had grown accustomed to going through this small village without bothering to reduce speed very much. I was soon to regret this practice, however, for as I was about to enter the second curve, I recall putting the headlights back on high beam and I was surprised to see so many reflectors in the middle of the road.

115

I tried the brakes, but since the old road was wet, I had to be careful not to go into a tail spin. As I got closer, I realized that a large herd of cows was on the road. In my whole life, I'd never seen so many cows in one bunch, and they looked more like milk-cows than the old white-faced cattle. As I started to enter the herd of cows, I began to wonder what I was going to tell the boss. I didn't give a single thought to my own safety. I knew the company would fry my hide for driving too fast for the road conditions, over-driving the headlights, not having the vehicle under control, plus about a dozen other things they would dream up.

Almost miraculously, the cows began to turn and split, some moving to the right, and some to the left. I recall that as I went by one old cow, I could literally see the whites of her eyes. I'll never know how, but I didn't hit a single cow, not because I so skillfully avoided it...it just happened! As I checked the passenger mirror, it seemed everyone was fast asleep, and luckily for them, they weren't even aware of what had almost happened.

Resuming speed on the trip, I couldn't keep my right foot on the accelerator without it jumping up and down, my hands were kinda' sweaty, and I found it very difficult to drive fast for the next few miles. Telling the other driver about the incident, he said the cows weren't on the road when he went by, but asked me how many I thought there were. I told him my estimate was at least a thousand.

Slow down on wet roads, Howard.

ANXIOUS LITTLE OLD LADY

Late one night going east from Amarillo to
Oklahoma City, I arrived in Elk City and parked at
the curb. The bus station was closed, but I noticed a
car parked there with people in it, so I assumed that
someone wanted to board the bus. I figured it was a
mother and daughter, and evidently my assumption
was correct, as the younger woman was trying to
slow the little older lady down a notch or two. The
older woman would pass for my own mother...in her
actions, anyway. She was dressed very nicely, hat
and all, her large black purse held in front of her
with both hands. As they approached the bus, I
started to joke with her a little. I was about ten

minutes ahead of schedule, so I might as well take it easy.

The old lady asked me, "Do you have any seats on that bus?" Kidding her a little, I said, "Yes 'em, in fact, I ain't never seen one of these here big ole' Greyhounds without any seats." She then snapped back, obviously not amused, "No, no! I mean, are you loaded?" I tried humor again, "Oh, no, ma'am, I didn't drink anything. In fact, I quit drinkin' twenty years ago and ain't had one since." At that point, the younger woman started laughing and put her arm around her mother and said, "Honey, can't you see he's teasin' you a little?" At that point, the older lady started laughing with us. I then took her by the arm, told her we had plenty of good seats left, in fact, she could have two seats together if she liked. Furthermore, she didn't have to change buses to get to her destination. She was delighted to hear this. I took her ticket.

Her daughter gave her a big kiss and hug, but as the older woman started to get on, I stated, muttering but being sure they heard me, "Boy, if that don't beat all. I stay up all night, do all the driving, and everybody in town gets hugged but me!" Well, guess what! They both started laughing and planted one on me, too. We all had a good laugh and we went merrily on our way. I even wound up with lipstick on my cheek. Oh, well! It's a tough job, but somebody had to do it. Be friendly, we're all alike.

THE DRIVER IS A GENIUS

Back in the early fifties on a very hot summer morning, I was given an assignment to take an extra section from Amarillo to Albuquerque. The passengers on the bus were unloaded at the terminal for a rest stop while the bus was taken to the shop to be serviced. The Oklahoma City driver told the mechanic that the bus had a very bad problem with overheating and, in his opinion, would not make the trip on to Albuquerque. The Amarillo dispatcher advised us that there was no other choice, as there was not other bus available and wouldn't be for five or six hours.

119

The mechanic did the best he could within the short period of time he had and everything seemed to check out. He did flush out the radiator and wished me "good luck" as I left the shop. The passengers were reloaded at the terminal and I departed toward 6th Street, which at that time was Route 66, passed through San Jacinto, past the Veterans Hospital, then on to Wilderado, Vega, Adrian, and off the caprock on down to Glen Rio, which sat right on the Texas-New Mexico state line. Here, there was always a short break for coffee before heading southwest to Bard and San Jon.

So far, the engine was doing all right, which wasn't too surprising, as the terrain was flat or slightly downhill. I thought I could probably make the few miles on to Tucumcari where there would be a rest stop and I could check the water level. So far, so good.

After lunch, we pulled back out on Route 66 and headed for the next rest stop at the Club Cafe in Santa Rosa. While having coffee, I remembered that the mechanic back in Amarillo had told me that the heat gauge might be sending a false signal; if so, it wouldn't hurt the engine to keep running. I asked him how this was to be accomplished if the automatic heat safety-valve cut the engine off. With a sly grin, he said, "You know, I'll get us both fired if I tell you that. Just remember what you learned in drivers' school about the skinner valve." Then I suddenly realized he was referring to a small, air-operated valve sitting atop the engine that would automatically cut off the fuel supply when the engine reached a dangerous temperature.

As I sat there, I knew that the trip so far was the easy part. From Santa Rosa to Albuquerque was 118 miles with numerous, long, steady, up-hill climbs and this was the middle of the afternoon and it was quite hot. Expecting the worst, I re-boarded the passengers and started out of Santa Rosa. Crossing the Pecos River, I was thinking, "Well, old girl, it's all uphill from here on!" Climbing out of Santa Rosa was no picnic back then, for usually slow traffic would hinder any attempt to gain speed, and as the road was single lane, passing was almost impossible.

About half-way up to the top of this long hill, the heat buzzer came on, emitting a fairly loud, screeching noise, along with flashing lights on the dash. Poor me! I hoped this thing would make it to the top before she blew, as I could see several large trucks and other vehicles following the black smoke being bellowed out by the bus. Luckily, we made it to the top and gained enough speed for me to try a higher gear, but that proved to be too much and the engine came to an abrupt halt. Oh well, at least here the traffic could get around us.

After parking off the pavement, I told the passengers to open all the windows for ventilation, got my gloves and small crescent wrench, and opened the engine compartment doors. That old diesel engine sure was hot. By this time, several passengers had gathered around the rear of the bus asking all kinds of questions, some legitimate, some down-right silly. One old lady asked me if her daughter would have to wait on her in Los Angeles?

121

I tried to be civil to her, but frankly, I wanted to walk up to her face and scream, "How the HELL, do I know?" I did manage to refrain. As I was leaning over the hot engine, trying to get my wrench on the small air line, I noticed a white-haired gentleman standing behind me who had been sitting at the front of the bus with his wife. He said, "Sir, is there anything I can do besides ask silly questions?" At that time, I came out for air and laughingly said, "It seems that you know people pretty well."

After successfully removing the air line from the valve, I could see the small plunger inside the valve that must be kept depressed in order for the engine to get fuel. We were told in Greyhound School in Dallas that a small round pebble might be placed there in order to let the engine get fuel. Looking around for a small round pebble probably appeared very stupid to the passengers watching. They probably figured I'd suffered a heat stroke. Finding the small stone was easy. I then put it inside the valve atop the plunger and screwed the air line back on so the air wouldn't escape. Then I knew it was time go give it a try. If this was successful, the engine would now re-start, but it couldn't be turned off until it reached the shop in Albuquerque, assuming it hadn't burnt up by then.

Telling the passengers to get aboard, I felt cocky, assured that the engine would, indeed, run. We climbed back into the bus. The buzzer and red lights were still active. Now was the time. I hit the starter button and the old engine roared alive, amid cheering and applause from the passengers. As I sat there, running up the engine and allowing air pressure to build up, I'll admit I felt about ten-feet tall. By then the engine was cool enough that the buzzer and red lights had cut off. We closed all the windows and pulled out for Albuquerque, about 110 miles away. About five miles later, the buzzer and red lights came on, but I could put up with that if the engine would just hold together until we got in.

The white-haired gentleman on the front seat, in broken English, kept raving to his wife about the genius driver and how he fixed that huge engine with a small BB-sized pebble. He was quite amazed at how I could be so smart. Of course, I didn't argue with him, but if someone hadn't taught me, I wouldn't have known.

As we sailed past Flying C Ranch and Clines Corner, we could see the Sandia Mountains in the distance. Thinking that an old bus, like an old cow, could smell the watering hole, we kept on a goin', past Longhorn Ranch to Moriarty, and even up Comers Hill in good shape. Reaching the summit at last, it was only eighteen more miles to the station and all down hill! Traffic was kind to us and we pulled into the station right on time.

The genius made it...like a rock!

THE VANISHING VODKA

After leaving Albuquerque one summer afternoon at 3:30 going east to Amarillo, everything went okay for about an hour. Then I noticed a gentleman who was seated in the second row on the lower level of the Scenicruiser starting to talk a little louder as we went along.

It was difficult for me to tell exactly who he was talking to, as I could not see him that well in the mirror. Finally, during one of his stories, I violated a rule by turning around to see if what I suspected was true. Yep, he was talking to himself. But he did notice me turning in my seat, and realizing that I was getting suspicious, he then slipped his bottle into a small zipper bag by his feet. The man looked to be about sixty years of age and was dressed a little above average for a long-distance bus trip. As he wasn't that far away from me, I asked him a direct question, "Sir, have you been drinking any alcoholic beverages?"

"Hell no!" was the reply, which again is very typical. Then I asked him if he had any in his possession, and again, he emphatically denied having a bottle of spirits. I informed him that if he got any louder, I would leave him in Santa Rosa. He again informed me that he had no booze. After my fairly stern warning, he settled down a bit and we went on to Santa Rosa, where we had our evening meal stop at the Club Cafe.

After discharging the passengers and baggage, I then reached up into the bus to get my log book. I noticed this gentleman's small zipper bag was laying on the floor by his seat, with the neck of the bottle protruding out. Slipping the bottle out of the bag, I saw that it was a bottle of Vodka about half full. I hid it under a shop rag and took it to the rear of the parking lot where I threw the bottle over a wall along-side the railroad tracks, then continued about my business.

After the rest stop, we loaded back on the bus and after counting the passengers, I pulled out of Santa Rosa. About five miles out, the gentleman told me that he had a complaint, and I asked him if it was urgent. If it would wait until we were in Tucumcari in less than an hour, there I would sit down with him and discuss his problem. I knew this would give him more time to sit and pout about his missing bottle. Upon arrival in Tucumcari, I told the man to go ahead and get some coffee and I would see him shortly. As soon as I could, I joined him at his table and asked him what the problem was. He sat up straight in his chair and told me that I hád violated his constitutional rights by removing his personal property and that I would be reported to the Interstate Commerce Commission, and my job would be in real jeopardy.

Turning over the bus shop card, which was a large manila-colored sheet with lines on it, and acting like I was filling out his report, I asked him to describe the property. He stuttered and stammered, and replied, "You know very well what I'm talking about." I said, "Sure I do, but when you go to prove it, which bottle are you going to say I took from you? The bottle you said you didn't have in the first place, or the one that I found after you lied to me, or maybe it wasn't yours in the first place?"

As I was getting only a stare at this point, I unloaded on him with both barrels about transporting illegal spirits across state lines, and how these small-town sheriffs would enjoy getting him, and how awful their jails were. Then, I suggested that if he wanted to continue on the bus, he would sit quietly without talking, read, sleep, or just look out the window; and the minute I heard him utter a word, he'd be hitch-hiking.

He understood. We made it fine the rest of the way. I imagine that he had been down that road before.

WHERE'S THE COURTHOUSE?

I was leaving Oklahoma City as the second section on the 5:00 p.m. schedule to Amarillo. Usually, the first bus was loaded with through-passengers to points beyond Amarillo, like Los Angeles, so the second section handled all the local passengers, making most of the stops along the way. As I arrived in Weatherford, about two hours out at 7:00 p.m., I stopped in front of the bus station. As I recall, I had four passengers off there, but only three had left the bus. Stepping back in the bus, I called out Weatherford again, but no one made a move. I then started to walk back into the rear of the bus to see if anyone might be sleeping, but no one was.

The only thing to do then was check everyone's ticket to see what their destination was. Finding an elderly gentleman with a big western hat and carrying a cane who had the ticket marked Weatherford, I asked him why he didn't want to get off. He was a little hard of hearing, but made up for it with volume and profanity when he spoke. He was looking around, sitting on the edge of his seat, bellowing out, "Where's the courthouse?" Finally, after several attempts, I made him understand that Weatherford had no courthouse.

He then exclaimed, "The hell it don't. I've been living there nigh on to sixty years, raised my family there, even had a niece who worked in the damned thing, so...by God...don't tell me, young feller, that Weatherford don't have a courthouse!" During the time it took for him to tell me this, I suddenly realized that he was probably going to Weatherford, Texas, which did have a courthouse. I finally got him in the station, which was a nice drug store with tables for eating.

After some research, I found out that he had a daughter in Ft. Worth, which was only forty miles east of Weatherford, Texas. He visited her quite frequently, but had been visiting another daughter in Oklahoma City, so it was easy to understand him being confused. He had told the ticket agent in Oklahoma City that he wanted a ticket to Weatherford. The agent, being particularly busy that day, assumed he meant Weatherford, Oklahoma.

We made arrangements to get him back to Oklahoma City and headed in the right direction. I've wondered many times about what a colorful story he had for his daughters, but then, on the other hand, she might have thanked us for giving him a 5 to 6 hour free ride. It might have been rather peaceful for them.

SOLDIERS TO ST. LOUIS

At Christmas time, Ft. Sill had chartered thirty buses from Ft. Sill to St. Louis. Most of these assignments were from Oklahoma City to St. Louis, as the Oklahoma City extra board was not that large, and traffic was very heavy on all other schedules. Manpower was at a premium. Having arrived in Oklahoma City in the early morning, I had already gotten my eight hours sleep when the dispatcher called me to report to the shop, wait for the buses to arrive from Ft. Sill, and then take one to St. Louis, a distance of about five hundred and twenty miles.

It was raining very hard when I took a cab to the shop about 5:00 p.m. and the weather report was

133

terrible--freezing rain, sleet, and high winds. About 7:00 p.m., we found out the bad weather had delayed the arrival of all thirty buses from Ft. Sill and they probably wouldn't be there until about midnight. All the drivers were lounging around the drivers' room, shooting pool, some trying to sleep, read, or whatever they could find to do. Most would rather have stayed in bed until the buses arrived. Like most bureaucracies, Greyhound and the Army were as bad as it could get. What Greyhound couldn't screw up, the Army could.

My son was in Oklahoma Christian at Edmond, so I thought this would be a good time to visit him and his wife, if they didn't mind driving to the shop. They arrived at the shop about 9:00 p.m. and we sat in the car and talked for an hour or so. My son commented about what a lousy night it was to have to go to St. Louis. I agreed one hundred percent, because to make matters worse, I didn't even know the way out of town. After our visit, I found a driver from Oklahoma City who agreed to lead me out to Turner Turnpike, but like everything else that night, even that got cross-threaded.

About midnight, the buses started rolling in. The soldiers remained on the buses while they were serviced and fueled. At that time, the next driver would move out toward St. Louis. The hotline to the dispatch office rang and the dispatcher gave me a bus number. It was such an odd number that after asking around, I found out it was an old bus that had been taken out of moth balls for the Christmas rush. In fact, it was so old that it had a six-cylinder engine

134

in it. All the remaining buses had the newer V-8 engines, which were quite peppy. I then discovered that I was the only "foreign" driver, being from Amarillo. The other drivers were from Oklahoma City or Tulsa. I also noticed that the old bus came in last.

Here I was, the oldest bus, icy road, and unfamiliar territory. Luckily, after the bus was serviced and I started to leave, there was the Oklahoma City driver waiting for me, and I certainly appreciated that, as he had to go slower than the rest in order for me to catch up. We finally made it to Turner Turnpike and headed for Tulsa. The driver leading me was just ahead of me. All the others had disappeared. Having no trouble keeping up on the ice, about forty miles out, the moon started to peer through the clouds, showing that the ice had begun to dissipate; in fact, the outside lane was completely clear of ice. That was a relief for sore eyes.

At that time, the bus ahead started going full speed, which back then was about seventy-two miles per hour. I was pushing as hard as I could, but I thought I'd seen the last of those guys. As I sat there feeling sorry for myself, I noticed the bus in front of me was slowing down, or was she? I looked at my speedometer and it was on eighty mph. I couldn't believe it. After checking the way I was catching up with him, it must have been correct. As I passed him, I felt sad about outrunning him, as he had been so nice to show me the way. I dropped back to his speed until our first coffee stop. I don't remember where it was on the turnpike; several of the other drivers were already there. He told me that the speedometer was correct, for he was going as fast as he could when I passed. While having coffee, he told me that if that old girl wanted to go to St. Louis, to let her go, even though she was older.

When we pulled out again, the other bus was in front of me by about two miles before I got mine wound up. By this time, there was no ice, the moon was out full, and I thought to myself, "Man, if this old girl holds together, I'll be in St. Louis long before any of the rest." Because I still had 400 miles to go, I wondered if some mechanic in Dallas thought, in order for this old bus to keep up, he'd better just turn the screw up on the governor a turn or two. If he did, I certainly appreciated that. After passing my friend, he blinked good luck. I could see several sets of marker lights ahead that turned out to be the other buses. Later, those guys told me they had felt sorry for me back in Oklahoma City and here I came, blowing them all off the road.

The extra speed also caused me to be more alert and made my old adrenaline flow so much that I was bright-eyed and bushy-tailed. As I recall, out of the thirty that had left ahead of me, only about four arrived in St. Louis ahead of me; which only reinforces that old saying, "Snow on the roof, but fire in the furnace!"

THE CRAZY HOP-HEAD

Late one afternoon, on a trip from Amarillo to Oklahoma City, everything seemed to be normal until reaching a small town called Alanreed. It seemed that a young man in the rear of the bus was feeling awful good--or maybe awful bad. After stopping the bus, I went back to see if there was a reason for all the commotion.

It seemed that the fellow was about half-crazy on something; as I couldn't smell liquor on his breath, I had to assume that he was on some type of drug, but of course, I couldn't find out what. One of his buddies assured me that he would keep him quiet, so we proceeded on to our first rest stop in

Shamrock. The fellow did fairly well until we got within about ten miles of our stop, when he started standing in the aisle, and shouting and raving. Instead of stopping again, I decided to keep a sharp eye on him and push on into Shamrock where I could get the police or sheriff to remove him from the bus.

As I parked at the station and announced to the passengers that we would be there thirty minutes, everyone seemed very relieved. After the passengers had gotten off the bus, I noticed the loud-mouth had chosen not to get off. It may have been because he had been refused transportation before, and probably not too far back. After calling the sheriff and finding out he was out of town--but would be back shortly, probably during our rest stop--I couldn't help but notice a very tall, slender fellow sitting at the end of the counter drinking coffee. He was wearing boots, a cowboy hat, had a gun on his belt, and was even wearing a badge. After introducing myself, and finding out he was a game warden, I told him my problems. He told me that he wasn't authorized as a peace officer in the usual sense, but if it would help, he would be glad to stand out by the door of the bus and say nothing. Expressing my thanks, I told him I thought that would be sufficient.

Before re-loading the bus, I was going to try and get the loud-mouth off, but when I got about ten feet from him and motioned for him to come off the bus, the profanity started. He started coming toward me and I started backing out...all the while telling him to get his belongings, this was the end of the line for him. Getting an old box out of the over-head baggage rack, he came off the bus full of words and threats that I dare not repeat.

When he stepped off the bus, he looked up with eyes that were glazed over, but instead of seeing me, he was looking straight at a long, hog-leg hanging on a wide black belt with lots of bullets in it. As the guy was fairly short, he stopped talking for the first time in about an hour. He looked up at this sun-tanned Texan with arms folded staring down at him. Standing there for a while, letting this scene soak into his drugged-up brain, I pointed toward the door of the bus station and he obeyed immediately. I told him to sit down and say nothing.

After re-loading the passengers, a waitress told me that the sheriff had called and was on his way. The game warden told me I could go ahead and he would stick around waiting for the sheriff to arrive. The sheriff in Shamrock, at that time, was fearless, quiet, very knowledgeable of everyone in the county, and what they were up to, but still courteous and friendly. After several weeks had passed, the sheriff told me that when he picked the person up that day, he took him to jail and let him sleep it off. Then the next day, he took the prisoner over to the bus station to buy him lunch with the intentions of releasing him; but, before leaving the jail this guy gave him and his deputy a good cussin'. The sheriff took him over for lunch anyway, and then told him that the jail needed a new coat of paint and that, if he worked hard and kept his nose clean, he should be able to continue on to New York in about three weeks.

The sheriff told the guy to stay there after he was through eating. He knew he wouldn't, and sure enough, when he returned, the guy was gone. The sheriff then proceeded to the "flats" and asked a bootlegger about a stranger. Naturally, it took only a few minutes to locate the prisoner. Back in those days, when the sheriff asked you something, you went along with it. The sheriff told me that he took the fellow back to the bus station to eat every day, and informed him that, if he decided to run, the outside of the jail needed painting, too, and it would take about an additional three weeks for that. He laughingly told us that the fellow wouldn't even leave the stool to go to the rest-room until he returned. The guy finally left town on a Greyhound bus on the twenty-second day after being introduced to the "Game Warden."

Often, I would wonder how far down the road the guy would get before he did it again. Times may be different, now, but I sometimes have to wonder if they're better.

THE BIG BLIZZARD

About 10:00 p.m. late one spring, in the midst of a snow storm, I was called to report to the shop. The wind was howling and the snow was getting quite heavy. Route 66 had been closed east of Amarillo for several hours, so the boss in Tulsa decided to send us down Route 60 to Panhandle, then south to Groom, since the road was supposed to be okay on east of there. My assignment that night was to be an extra section, along with several others, so as to clear the Amarillo station of a backlog of passengers.

After taking the Scenicruiser to the station and loading it to capacity, we started out. We made it fairly well to Panhandle, turned south to Route 66, then east for only a short distance where we found lines of traffic stalled on both the east and west lanes of Route 66. Since we couldn't proceed any further, we sat on the bus with the engine running until daylight. The wind was blowing very hard, and it was impossible to really tell what was going on. I could see I was directly behind an eighteen-wheeler and directly behind me were two more loaded Scenicruisers.

Bus passengers rarely prepare for any kind of trouble or emergencies. There were two or three young mothers with small children who were running out of milk, baby food, etc. Needless to say, everyone was getting kinda' fidgety as there was no room to move around and only one seat per person. During the night, I tried to get a little nap, but found the only way I could get sleepy was when the bus was moving!

One fellow on the bus had a radio, so we could at least get weather conditions, which were not too good. They kept telling us the snow plows were coming, but as the wind was very high, they weren't doing much good. There were a couple of ladies from Arkansas on the front seat, and they melted snow for anyone who wanted water. They were very helpful in any way they could be.

About mid-morning, I put on my parka and walked back to the other buses to check on them. They were doing about the same as we were. I returned to my bus and told the two ladies that I had seen a jack-rabbit pushing another to get him

142

started. That turned out to be the slogan of the day, and we had some fun with one another. As best I could tell, the snow was only about six inches deep, but it was very wet and heavy, accompanied by a high wind. Our location was about three-fourths of a mile east of a very small store and grain elevator called Lark. The tall grain elevators could be seen once in a while at Groom, but they were about six miles away...and it might as well have been a hundred miles under these circumstances...we just couldn't get there.

About mid-afternoon, the driver directly behind me came to my bus and suggested that he and I walk back to the small store and see if perhaps we could obtain some food. If we found them closed, we could force entry, leave our names and a record of what we "stole." As this was a spring storm, and the temperature wasn't all that cold, the walk to the store was not bad because we had a line of eighteen-wheelers for wind breaks for part of the way. Luckily, the little store was still open, but didn't have much stock. The other driver and I bought up everything we could get that was ready to eat. The little lady was very helpful as she accepted our check and as the little store looked rather dismal, probably most of the motorists did not know she was open.

The driver in the third bus in line was not informed much about the weather conditions, so he stayed with all three buses while we were gone. He had no boots or parka. We returned to the buses a couple of hours later and distributed the food among them as equally as possible. My food was a small box of raisins and a few Fig-Newtons. Once the food was distributed, I walked up to the eighteen-wheelers in front of me. The two drivers had been quite helpful to us. When I knocked on the door, the sleeping drivers rolled the window down, and I handed them the Fig-Newtons. It surprised me that they took only one cookie each. They were so considerate that, when I told them they could have the whole package, which wasn't all that large, the one by the window said, "You mean the whole ___ _____ package?"

After returning and while eating my raisins, I listened to the radio; it didn't sound good. They were reporting that since the Rock Island Railroad was parallel to the highway, they were sending out a snow-plow and some cars to pick up the stranded travelers. About an hour later, they announced the railroad plow had encountered drifts that it just couldn't handle with the available equipment. Not long after that announcement, a group of men approached the bus. Most had shovels and the one leading the pack was the one I'd given the cookies to. He told me that about a dozen of the truck drivers were going to shovel me out so the buses could get to town. Asking, "Why me?", he replied, "By God, anybody that will walk through this mess and gives us food, deserves the best." So, he had rounded up the other men to help.

They told me to go around the other vehicles and every time the bus would stall, they'd shovel it out. If successful, maybe we could all eventually make a trail. After sticking several times during this attempt, we made it to the front of the stalled traffic.

Again, I stalled, and after the truckers shoveled out some more snow, they asked me to step outside. The drive wheels were spinning in mid-air. The snow had packed so much that the wheels didn't touch the road. The bus had, as one driver put it, "made a belly landing." We were definitely stuck this time, until something could pull us off the packed snow underneath. The men worked their hearts out, but to no avail. They finally returned to their own vehicles.

The passengers were now fully awake and excited about the prospects of getting to town. After telling them what had transpired, they quieted down to a hush, and the lady from Arkansas said, "Well, at least we have ringside seats, now that we're first in line." As the wind would subside occasionally, we could see the elevators in Groom, and a farm house off to the right about a mile away. As anyone who lives in this country knows, you try walking in a blizzard only as a last resort because of the wind chill. It's even possible to "drown" with so much moisture moving in the air.

By that time, we had been stuck on the bus for about eighteen hours. Thank God we had snow for water and the bus was filled with fuel in Amarillo. Diesel engines will fast-idle for several days when not moving. The bus had a restroom, which was beginning to get a little rank by now, because of its low chemical capacity and most of us had gotten a bite or two of food today; but it could have been worse. The babies were getting tired and hungry, but it seemed that when you put us "ole, ornery Americans" in a pinch, we buckle down and help anyone; especially young mothers with children.

About 4:00 o'clock that afternoon, some man knocked on the door. He stepped into the bus and asked how far away the town was. I told him about five miles. He was stranded behind us in a fancy sport car of some kind and he told us he was going to walk to town. After I asked him for his reason, he stated that maybe he could be of some help. I told him, if he was out of gas, he and his family were welcome to come aboard the bus. He then informed me that he was tired of getting the run-around from the officials of this "hick state" and his intentions were to walk to town, call the governor, and give him a piece of his mind.

Of course, this was ridiculous, but where he came from, "they had snow-plows and cared for their people." I asked him, if he did make it to town, what in the world he'd tell anyone that they didn't already know? I told him that we'd been listening to the radio and that the plows were practically useless at this time on account of the wind. The best thing at this time, was to stay in the vehicles. He was determined to go and tell somebody off, so I opened the door and he disappeared toward town, leaning into the wind at about a forty-five-degree angle.

After the guy left, a trucker stopped in to ask about the farm house and the possibility of obtaining a tractor. Again, I tried to explain that if he made it and found them home, he could enjoy some food, some sleep, and the comforts of home, but that a farm tractor in this situation would be useless. He felt that he should try it anyway. I then asked him if he would like to borrow my water-proof parka, since it had a hood. He gladly accepted, with the provision that he would leave it in town at the truck stop. He, too, disappeared into the snow, heading toward the farm house. I never saw him again.

Not remembering how much time had passed, I noticed another figure leaning into the wind, almost falling occasionally, approaching the bus from the east. The lady on the front seat was elated, hoping he could be of some help. As he came closer, I opened the bus door, and he fell into the step-well. Frost had formed on his nostrils, eyelashes, and whiskers. While waiting for him to catch his breath, we noticed that he was the man in the fancy sports car. After determining that he was going to be okay, the lady from Arkansas leaned forward and asked him, "Sir, did you talk with the governor?" The man only grunted and departed for his car. It was probably lucky for him that he saw his mistake and returned before it was too late.

Just before sunup, the radio announced the railroad plow had arrived in Groom from the east with a passenger car. At about the same time, one of the passengers noticed a yellow, flashing light approaching from the direction of town. Then, the cab came into view, and lo and behold, it was a snow plow! The wind had subsided some, and they were making another attempt. They approached the bus, asked where to hook on, turned the plow around, and pulled me forward off the snow. They then unhooked, turned around and waved. Man, I put that ole' cruiser in gear, and amidst a lot of cheering and yelling, we went to town.

In Groom, it seemed that every farmer in the country with any kind of tractor with blades, was out working to get traffic moving. The first thing I wanted to do was stop at the local truck stop and let everyone eat. But, after calling the dispatcher, he informed me that the train was waiting at the station to take all the bus passengers. Then, I was to be sure and fuel up, and deadhead the buses on to Oklahoma City. As I was using the phone, I noticed a solid stream of traffic coming through from the west, including the other two buses. I guess, after they got me out of the way, the trail was open and all the rest were allowed to come through.

After informing the other drivers of the dispatcher's orders, we unloaded all the passengers at the train station, fueled the three buses, then proceeded east on Route 66, noticing all the while that the road was improving. By the time we got to Shamrock, the road was clear. This was so typical of a panhandle spring blizzard.

We stopped in Sayre for coffee. By then, the roads were completely dry; in fact, the sand was blowing. As we sat, feeling dirty and scruffy, a tourist walked up to us and asked how the roads were on west Route 66. As the snow and ice had melted off the buses by then, I didn't think he believed us. One of the Oklahoma drivers, who was fairly worn-out by then, turned on his stool, looked up at the man and asked him why he bothered to ask. Why didn't he just go find out for himself?

Upon arrival in Oklahoma City, a shower and a bed were certainly welcome sights.

After thinking about this incident later, I decided that if I ever got into any trouble on the highways of America, I wouldn't mind at all having them "smokin', chewin', spitting', cussin', truck drivers on our side. Believe me, you could sure do a lot worse.

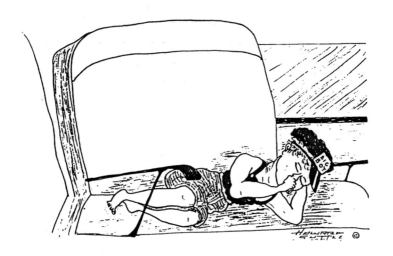

TODDLER MISSING

Late one evening, as we were pulling into the parking lot of the Club Cafe in Santa Rosa, I noticed that a westbound Scenicruiser was just pulling out for Albuquerque. The second section of that schedule was still there, and I had a second section coming behind me. This left three buses out on the parking lot. It was summer time, and just before the buses started coming in, a young couple with a three-year old boy traveling by car had stopped there, too.

While we were having our meal, we noticed some highway patrol units had pulled up and were talking with the excited couple. In just a minute or two, one of the owners came over to our table and asked if we would mind looking in our buses for the toddler. It seemed the mother thought her husband had him, so she started looking around the gift shop; the husband, thinking that the toddler was with his mother, had overlooked the little boy for a short time, and now he was missing. Everyone looked every place they could think of, but he was not to be found. As it came time to leave, we let the parents inside the buses to satisfy them that no one traveling on the bus had taken him.

Later that day, after all the buses had left, Phil, one of the coffee shop owners, suddenly remembered that one of the westbound buses had departed for Albuquerque before the parents realized there was a problem. That paid off. The highway patrol called ahead and had this particular bus stopped, about sixty miles up the road. The driver was not aware of the problem, but he went back on the bus and found the toddler curled up in a double seat, sound asleep. Evidently, all the passengers had assumed he belonged to someone on the bus.

Needless to say, the message that came over the radio was exciting news for everyone. As the parents were going west anyway, they met the patrol at Clines Corners and found him still asleep, only this time curled up in a patrol car. Too bad every missing child case doesn't turn out this happily.

HELP FROM OLE' BENNIE

One summer in the early fifties, I was still fairly new on the job. We had gotten very busy and all the extra men were scrambling for a day off. About the only thing we saw was the white line down the highway, and occasionally a bed. The summers were the busiest, and wouldn't you know, that's the time that friends and relatives came by for a visit. If a person has never worked all hours of the day and night, they just don't understand, of course. Ours was not a job where you could take a short nap down at the office. This is a story that I think of as typical for a new driver.

I arrived in Amarillo one afternoon about 4:00 o'clock, and the summer days being long, it wouldn't get dark until about 9:30 in the evening. Arriving home to find some family members from out of town, I visited and we had a good time. Suspecting that I would be called as soon as my eight hours were up, I hoped I could get some sleep, since maybe things were letting up. About 9:00 p.m., I excused myself and went to bed. If you've ever tried it, you know how difficult it is to go to sleep when it is still daylight. Kids are still playing, dogs are barking, and your neighbors are barbecuing outside. Knowing full well that you must sleep, it seems impossible. I finally dropped off around 10:00 p.m., and wouldn't you know, at midnight the dispatcher called and told me I would be going to Oklahoma City.

As I was backing out of the driveway, noticing that all my relatives, the kids, and, in fact, the whole neighborhood was sound asleep, I couldn't help wondering if every hoot-owl driver didn't indulge in a little self-pity. By the time I was loaded and had left town, it was about 1:00 a.m. I was the third section; in other words, it took three buses to handle the people on that one schedule.

By the time I got to the first rest stop, which was Shamrock, I was feeling pretty dull. I had heard that if you mix coffee and coke, it would keep you awake. After taking two or three cups of this concoction, I headed out. The front two buses were about fifteen minutes ahead of me, so I didn't even have any tail-lights to follow. Poor me!

After passing Erick, heading east, I thought I was doing fairly well until I saw this hay truck in front of me with no tail lights. After I hit the brakes, which rolled a baby or two out of their seats, plus sent cans and bottles rolling down the aisle, I woke up enough to notice the hay truck turned out to be a bush that had been planted at the end of a small culvert. Man, it hit me then and there, that I was in no shape to drive. It's very difficult to lay off in the western part of Oklahoma at 3:30 in the morning, and back in those days, there wasn't anything open all night.

Evidently, the good Lord was doing the driving, because we caught up with the first two buses at the breakfast stop in Clinton. As I sat there drinking coffee with the driver just ahead of me, I told him of my predicament. He then told me not to eat anything and slipped me a small pill or capsule. I frankly don't remember the size or color of what he gave me, but he told me to chew it up, drink about two more cups of coffee with it, and I would have fast results. He was right. After all, he was an expert, I found out later. This fellow took pills to stay awake, pills to go to sleep, and drank gin in between. Come to think of it, I realized later that I had never known of his actually eating food. Needless to say, this man was eventually fired from his job and died fairly young.

Well, back to "The Pill." It was called a "Bennie"--short for Benzedrine--and was probably strong enough to be referred to by truck drivers as an "LA turn-around." That phrase suggested that a person could leave Oklahoma City and pull an LA turn-around without getting sleepy. Boy, do I ever believe it! He told me that I would have no trouble getting to Oklahoma City, which was about two and a half hours away, and upon arrival, I should be sure to eat a good breakfast and then I would be able to sleep--the food was to kill the effect.

Baloney! Here's what happened, and I do well remember! After chewing the bitter pill in Clinton, I loaded my passengers about sunrise, pulled out onto Route 66, and headed east. At that time, the old road crossed an old steel bridge that had timber as a floor. I can still remember the old planks rattling as I crossed. As I came off the bridge, the whole world opened up. It felt as if my eyes literally popped open. The narrow Oklahoma road seemed like a real wide, smooth freeway. It was kinda' frightening, for I thought I had died and gone to heaven (and I really hadn't expected it to be that way!). It was such a relief not to have to fight the battle of sleepiness. The large wooden steering wheel felt like it was about the size of a doughnut, and the hills were no problem, either. I could see the butterflies on the bushes half a mile away and I could have driven that big bus through that doughnut steering wheel.

The old gasoline engine ran so quietly, and I was feeling so good, that I thought, "Boy, I could go all the way to St. Louis, if they wanted me to." Upon arrival in Oklahoma City, we had several railroad crossings, and when I arrived at the first one, it was "procedure" to stop and open the passenger door before proceeding. As I found out later, most people didn't understand why, so I'll clarify. We were taught to come to a complete stop, open the passenger door before crossing, and listen, as well as look, for on-coming trains. We were to cross the tracks only in first gear, never shifting gears, or closing the door until the tracks were cleared, because shifting the gears would increase the possibility that the clutch, drive-line, or engine would be more likely to fail. If the bus stalled on the tracks, and a train was approaching, you wouldn't risk the possibility of a load of people stacking up against a closed door; it would already be open.

When people asked us why we did this, most drivers would kid them a little, saying it was to let the train through or so the driver could get out faster. We had some fun with this one.

Back to the first crossing. I came to a stop, looked both ways as usual, started to reach for the door handle, but couldn't get my hand over to it. I was so weak and nervous my arm was very slow to respond; so for the rest of the crossings, I only stopped and looked.

I was in quite a hurry to get unloaded so I could get across the street and get a good breakfast, then go to the hotel and hit the ol' sack. But I soon found out what that drug could do to me. As I lay in bed for what seemed like an eternity, closely examining the cracks in the ceiling (which resembled some sort of road map), I dropped off to sleep every once in a while; but, the old hay truck and other things would reappear and I would wake up startled.

It was very difficult to separate reality from dreaming and I doubt if I slept over twenty-minutes in my eight hours off. Finally, I just got up, went down to eat again, and later drove all the way back to Amarillo, without drowsiness. In fact, after I got home, I still couldn't sleep.

It took about a week for the effects of that one pill to wear off and my life to return to normal. During the week of recovery, I decided once and for all that, in order to hold a job like this, one must consider himself first and get his rest--regardless of company, relatives, or friends. One thing for sure, I would never swallow, snort, shoot, inhale, or even think about indulging in anything that would alter my mind. I think that is why I made it for twenty-eight more years with only a few normal problems.

That incident taught me that under the influence of ole' "Bennie" or what-ever it was, my reaction time was a lot slower than normal. Finding out that the good effects were all a big lie, I also learned that the come-down was pure hell. It's easy to understand how so many people can get hoodwinked. After all, the devil gives no bargains. True, for two or three hours the steering wheel gets small, the road gets smooth and wide, the engine runs quietly, and you feel like you can smell the roses fifty miles away; but the days of no sleep to speak of, loss of appetite, and nervousness sure weren't worth it. That's when I realized, it's much better to go to bed.

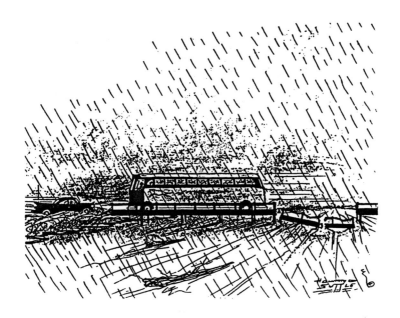

BRIDGE OUT AT
SAYRE, OKLAHOMA

One morning, coming back to Amarillo from
Oklahoma City, the trip was fairly routine, but I
noticed that the area must have had quite a rain the
night before. As we were leaving Sayre, heading
west on old Route 66, we approached the long,
narrow bridge crossing the north fork of the Red
River. We noticed that the river was still running
fairly full. The water was high and had turned red
with mud, as it usually does after a rain. We were
stopped for a short time before being allowed to cross
the bridge which had been fitted with a temporary
span--made of some sort of army equipment, similar
to loading ramps on cargo planes-- replacing a

portion of bridge that had washed out the night before. The one-way-at-a-time crossing was slow, but the delay wasn't too bad. A day or two later, I asked another Amarillo driver if he was aware of the bridge being washed out. This is his story.

Two nights previously, he was the third section from Oklahoma City to Amarillo. As he crossed the bridge, it was raining heavily. He was meeting a car that wouldn't dim its headlights. He said when he met the car shortly after he came off the bridge, he noticed that it appeared to be a black Cadillac. He recalled that certain models of Cadillac were equipped with automatic dimmer devices, which in a rain storm might not work.

After he arrived in Shamrock about an hour later, he was told that the bridge at Sayre was washed out, and this could possibly have happened just after the three buses crossed over. Authorities couldn't find out if any vehicle had plunged into the water. At the time we both wondered how the authorities had found out about the bridge washing out. We later discovered that the black cadillac had been found several miles downstream with the body of a man inside.

The other driver said that every time he thought of this, it would give him the shivers, even more than when he flew bombers in WW II. On subsequent trips, we could see under the old bridge and see that cement had been poured over timbers driven into the sandy river bed. Needless to say, it was very spooky going over this bridge, especially on dark, rainy nights. Years later, I-40 was a welcome alternative.

THE STATELY GENTLEMAN
FLIPS OUT

Late one evening, I was waiting in the
Oklahoma City station for the westbound schedule to
load. If it were to overload, I had a bus available to
me and was to go behind him. This is what we call
"protecting the schedule." As it turned out, the first
driver had about three seats left, with some getting
off at El Reno, so the dispatcher told me to ride back
with him to my home station of Amarillo.

As it turned out, I sat next to a middle-aged
lady from Clinton who was a nurse. We were seated
in the second seat behind the driver. Directly in
front of us sat a woman next to the window and next

to the aisle was a very smartly dressed, older gentleman, complete with stiff-brimmed black hat, and a black vest and coat, bow tie, walking cane, and a gold chain hanging from his vest pocket, suggesting he had a pocket watch inside. As the nurse and I started to visit casually, we couldn't help but notice the two directly in front of us engaged in no form of conversation and, therefore, must have been strangers.

Things went well, until we crossed the long, steel bridge over the Canadian River west of El Reno. The bridge is just a little short of a mile long, and as we proceeded on toward Hydro, we noticed the old gentleman starting to sit on the edge of his seat, looking straight down the road. The driver was keeping a close watch on him, too. Looking in the passenger mirror, the driver caught my eye, frowned and rolled his eyes. I was getting the message that he was concerned about the man.

When the old man put his right foot into the aisle while keeping his left hand on the rail behind the driver, I realized he was about to make some sort of move. But, of course, he could have been going merrily back to the restroom in the rear of the bus, which it is perfectly all right to do. However, something told me that he had something else in mind, as he never took his eyes off the road. Suddenly, he jumped up and grabbed the door handle. Immediately, I moved into the aisle and got on top of him, managing to keep him from opening the passenger door.

The nurse asked the lady on the front seat to trade seats with her and she gladly accepted. We decided that it would be better for her to sit beside him and try talking with him. I would stay directly behind him so I could hold his shoulders back when necessary. The old man started accusing the driver of taking him too far, saying he wanted off. He said he had passed his house about six blocks back and his wife would be worried if he was late. The nurse was very good at keeping him relatively calm until we made our stop in Weatherford. We finally convinced him that his wife, whose name the nurse had found out, would be waiting for him at the next stop. The driver wanted to get him to Clinton where we would have access to police, ambulance, and a hospital. Weatherford was just too small to handle a situation like this. While stopped at the station, the driver called ahead to the agent at Clinton, so the police could meet the bus. As we pulled into the driveway, the driver had already announced to the passengers that this was a thirty-minute meal stop.

As the police were standing there waiting to ask the gentleman a few questions, he started screaming and striking at the policemen with his cane. The cops then called for an ambulance on the radio, but until it arrived, it took four cops, two Greyhound drivers, and one nurse to contain the little old man. His strength was amazing, and his cane was also quite effective until it was removed from his possession.

After the ambulance arrived, and he was finally strapped down, one of the cops remarked, "I'll tell you one thing, if that old boy had a twin brother, by damn, we woulda' lost this battle." All of us had to agree. The police later told us that the gentleman was okay after some rest, but it turned out he was eighty-six years young, his wife had been gone for several years, and this was just another case of riding too far without resting. The driver then got the nurse's name, and told me that the next day he would order a dozen roses sent to her. I'll bet she would appreciate that.

Love thy neighbor!

AT FACE VALUE

One evening, I was taking a regular driver's run from Amarillo to Albuquerque. This was before we had a PA system or a rest room, so the procedure was to get all the passengers on board and seated. After closing the door, the driver was to stand in the front of the bus, facing the people, and make the necessary announcements, such as: next rest stop, arrival times, and other information covering the next few hours of travel. Then people would know where they would have meals, plus a few safety tips.

This particular evening, as I was checking tickets, a little old lady started informing me that the ticket agent in Chicago told her certain things that were completely false. After I started joking with her and assuring her that everything would be all right, she started to relax and we laughed a little about the situation. After loading the passengers, as I was closing the door, I couldn't help but overhear her telling her traveling companion about that lying agent.

As I stood there in the front of the bus, asking for everyone's attention, I made all the necessary announcements. I then looked down at her and in about a half-tone asked if anyone had any questions...if so, I would lie to them like all the ticket agents do. Everyone laughed, especially the lady with the complaint. We started laughing and having a good time, and it turned out to be a very enjoyable trip, with one exception.

The lady passenger turned out to be a "checker." This is a person hired by the company to check on a driver's performance. Sometimes they worked for Pinkerton or another professional detective agency, and the driver would never know where or when they would be on his bus. In about two weeks, the boss called me on the carpet to discuss an announcement I had made containing the statement: quote, "I will lie to you like all the ticket agents," unquote. There was nothing in the report about this being a joking matter, or that the lady had received some attention and ultimately enjoyed the trip. The boss let me go with the usual slap on the wrist kind of thing...for he, too, had been a driver.

It has always been a mystery to me where the company gets such brittle robots, without any emotions, and a complete lack of compassion. Oh well, that's bureaucracy for you.

TIED UP AT
HINTON JUNCTION, OKLAHOMA

It seemed like this particular winter Oklahoma had more ice storms than usual. This day was during one of those storms. About 6:00 o'clock one evening, I was in the hotel in Oklahoma City when the dispatcher called me to work. As I was leaving the hotel, I could see that this could very well be one of those long nights. Since everything was iced over, even walking the one block to the station was an ordeal in itself. Thinking, "Here we can hardly stand up, but we're running buses up and down the highways." Poor me! At this point, I sure envied a train engineer; at least he had tracks to run on.

At the station, the dispatcher told me to go behind the station and find a certain numbered bus. We always used numbers for positive identification. The dispatcher advised me that a driver had had a minor accident earlier in the day with the bus, and the passenger door had been damaged. I was to deadhead the empty bus to Amarillo, because we had a major shop there at that time. Using the back emergency door to board the bus, I noticed the front passenger door had been wired shut, leaving a gap about four inches wide from top to bottom. Since I was going west and the wind was from the north, I realized that this was going to be a very cold ride.

Starting out from Oklahoma City, I found the roads to be only wet. They were not icy at that time, but the night was young. Being pleasantly surprised that the heater and defroster were more than adequate, I had in fact decided to remove my jacket, thinking this might not be as bad as expected.

Wrong! About twenty miles west of El Reno the old Route 66 gets very hilly and those old curbs didn't help much either. One of the worst things about the curbs was that if a driver of any kind of vehicle happens to hit the right curb a little too hard, especially on ice, the force could rebound the vehicle back into oncoming traffic. Noticing that the steering wheel started to turn with exceptional ease, I knew I was in trouble. Since we had no power steering then, it meant I was running on solid ice.

By the time I arrived at the Canadian River, I began to notice highway trucks spreading sand and the long Canadian River Bridge had been sanded, so it was fine. After clearing the bridge, I was back on clear ice again, but in another two miles or so, I would stop at Hinton Junction for coffee at a twenty-four-hour truck stop. Arriving there, I noticed a roadblock just beyond the junction, so I had ample time for several cups of coffee. There were so many trucks parked all around that I could hardly find a parking place for the bus.

The cafe looked as if it were back in WW II years with "troops" lying all around trying to get a little snooze. Every stool was taken, and all booths and tables were occupied with four or five people crowded around them. People were leaning against the walls, the floor was covered with truck drivers and a few motorists. One driver, noticing that I had just arrived, gave me his stool so I could get a bite to eat and some coffee. The truck driver said the roadblock had been up several hours and the highway patrol said it would be after daybreak before the road would be opened. It was only 10:00 p.m.

After eating and returning to the bus, I noticed how nice and warm the bus was. Thinking that all those truck drivers would probably like a soft, reclining seat, I went back inside and approached a booth packed with truck drivers trying to sleep sitting up. I told the drivers that I had an empty bus that I had to keep running, and that if they wanted to sleep in a reclining seat, they were welcome. The drivers decided that anything would be better than those straight-backed booths. They told others about my offer. The cafe was almost

171

instantly cleared and all made a bee-line to the rear door of that bus. After everyone had settled down, I overheard a driver tell another that this was first class, and not to wake him till the sun came out. Since I was not as tired as they were, I returned to the cafe for another cup of coffee. There were only about three people left there.

Returning to the bus about midnight, I quietly found an empty seat and went to sleep. About daybreak, I woke up and went inside for a coffee eye-opener. The highway patrol arrived soon after, and told us that the weather was supposed to improve; and if things looked better about 10:00 a.m., they would possibly lift the roadblock. By this time, several truck drivers had come in from the bus and expressed their pleasure for their accommodations during the night. After enjoying a good breakfast, as most of the others were doing, I proceeded to the cashier to pay. She said it was already paid for. Not knowing who had done that, I waved and thanked them all.

Soon after breakfast, the blockade was removed and all the truckers let me go out first. It seemed that for the next few days, the truckers were extra-friendly when I met them on the highway. Maybe it was just coincidence, or perhaps some remembered the accommodations Hinton Junction's GREYHOUND HOTEL!

THE SCREWTAIL PUPPY

One summer evening, I was the second
section on the 5:00 o'clock local from Oklahoma City
to Amarillo. The bus was parked at an angle facing
the plate-glass of the bus station window. While I
was taking tickets at the door of the bus, I noticed in
the reflection of the glass a lady standing in line with
a small, screwtail bulldog puppy neatly tucked under
a sweater. As it was illegal to allow pets of any kind
(seeing-eye dogs were the only exception), she
thought she had the little dog covered fully from my
view, but hadn't considered the glass reflection.

The poor little puppy was shaking, her ears
laid back, and those black eyes looking like she

might be saying, "Please, sir, please. I want to go home." Seeing that little face reminded me of our own son's screwtail named "Boots." As the lady got up to me, I noticed she was only going a short distance to Clinton just two hours away. Her sweater was not out of place, because a lot of women carried them for night wear and in case they became chilly on the bus. Letting her board, I was quite careful to not notice anything different (after all, I had learned not to look for trouble, since trouble had no problem finding you without you looking for it).

As she stepped off the bus in Clinton, I whispered to her, "Nice puppy, Lady." She held her hand in front of her mouth and said, "You knew it didn't you?" I told her not to ask, to just enjoy the pretty little thing. The pup never made a sound. The lady said, "God bless you, sir; my little girl will love you for it!" The Three-Monkey Principle worked again!

MONEY LAUNDERING

Departing Albuquerque at 3:30 p.m., I was en route to Amarillo with a full double-decked Scenicruiser which had a rest room located on the lower level. About twenty miles out of Santa Rosa, I noticed a nicely dressed young man come out of the rest room, but instead of going back upstairs to his seat, he came up to me. In a very low and shy voice, he said he'd like to talk to me. I asked what I could do for him. He then told me that he had just dropped his wallet in the toilet and asked what he should do. Noticing that he had on a nice jacket, I told him the first thing to do was to remove the jacket, roll up his sleeves as far as possible, reach down and try to find his wallet. He then turned a little pale, so I explained to him that it was a chemical unit and couldn't be drained until we got to our shop in Amarillo, about four hours later.

Not being familiar with federal pollution laws, he thought maybe I could just pull over someplace and pull the plug. After I explained that this was strictly against the law, he was more willing to listen to my prediction that, if he waited until we arrived at the shop in Amarillo, the wallet may be dissolved by the chemicals. Telling him that, while I didn't want to appear smart or crude, the only thing he could reasonably do would be to fish it out, wrap it in paper towels, then wash himself with soap and water which we had on the bus. While in Santa Rosa for the meal stop of about forty minutes, he could thoroughly wash and dry his money and any other contents of the wallet. Trying to add a little humor, I told him that after his fishing expedition, he probably wouldn't have much of an appetite, anyway.

Laughingly agreeing, he went inside the toilet to see if his wallet was biting, so to speak. It took him only a couple of minutes to find it. Then after eating washed up, he returned to his seat, clutching his prize in a paper towel. After my meal, I went to the men's room at the Club Cafe and found the young man had washed his money and wallet and had them spread out over the stall dividers. After giving him all the time I could, I informed him that we must go. I returned to the bus, counting the passengers. He came up looking as good as new and very pleased that he had retrieved his money and wallet. As he stepped aboard, he grinned kinda' sheepishly and remarked, "Sir, you were right. I kinda' lost my appetite for awhile." This might be a story he would tell his grandchildren someday.

THE TRAILWAYS COMEDIAN

Tucumcari was a regular Greyhound rest stop for as long as I can remember. Our competitor, Trailways, also had a rest stop there, but their schedule would also change drivers. There was a small building out in the back of the station where the (Trailways) drivers could get some rest while waiting to return to either Amarillo or Albuquerque.

One of their drivers who drove from Albuquerque to Tucumcari, after several hours layover, would take another bus back to Albuquerque. This driver spent quite a bit of his time in the bus station, cutting up with the drivers and waitresses. This fellow had literally missed his calling, for he could keep more people laughing than any professional I had ever seen. He could act like an old lady and it would really crack you up. I know it's hard to explain, but I'll try. He'd put a napkin on his head and act like an old lady trying to put on lipstick with his small, black eyes crossed. It was hilarious.

Then, after that routine, he would hop across the coffee shop with his hands tucked under his arms, flapping his elbows, eyes crossed, and speech slurred, going south like Gertrude (an old Red Skelton routine), and people would almost cry with laughter. Well, needless to say, he enjoyed making people laugh, but early one night, he took it a little too far. His bus had arrived and his people had returned to the bus after a rest stop. He was sitting in his seat, ready to drive off, and the previous driver was standing in the doorway talking to him. He faked one of his seizures, jokingly, of course, but the other driver who was telling about this said it looked so real that he even he was convinced.

He said the fellow straightened out, started quivering with his tongue hanging out, eyes crossed, and his feet kicking the front of the bus. By this time, some of the passengers had gotten off and somebody had called the medics. Then, the would-be comedian, seeing he had gone to far, stood up, straightened his tie, and started laughing and explaining it was a joke. It turned out that several older ladies wouldn't ride any further. They said anybody who's that crazy shouldn't be driving anyway. I hear that the company got a little rough on him for that one.

We got news later that this driver's neighbor was working on his car when it fell on him. I heard that the driver lifted it up by himself enough for the fellow to get out, but in doing so, he was ruptured so badly that he later died. We were certainly saddened over this, but the laughter that he helped create will long be remembered by many. I'll just bet that, whatever cloud he occupies, he'll have somebody laughing, probably still taking ole' Gertrude south.

LUNCH FOR THE TRUCKER

One day, as I was en route from Amarillo to Albuquerque, we were having our regular lunch stop at the Club Cafe in Santa Rosa. Phil, one of the owners, sat at the booth I was in and asked me if I would do him a favor. Of course, I would, for he and his partner had fed drivers for free for years. I couldn't think of anything I wouldn't try to do for them.

He told me that another driver had advised him of a truck driver who had broken down about five miles east of the large Clines Corners restaurant and tourist stop. He told me the truck was an auto-hauler, and the driver had worked on the rig for several hours, but found it needed a part that had to be ordered. The driver caught a ride with a Greyhound to Clines Corners, but was refused service, no doubt because of his appearance. Not knowing how the news got back to Phil, I nevertheless assured him I'd be more than glad to stop. He put together a sack lunch and asked me to stop and give it to the driver.

About an hour and a half later, I spotted the broken-down truck and pulled around the truck and parked. The driver was waving for me to go on, as he knew I couldn't be of any help. Walking back, I talked with him for a minute, then asked if he had, indeed, been refused service at Clines Corners. It was true, but the very colorful way he had of describing the people who operated the place certainly wouldn't be appropriate for print.

After I gave him the sack, and told him who had sent it, he opened it and laid out the contents: the largest roast beef sandwich I'd ever seen, a pack of chips, and a huge slice of apple pie. To top it off, Phil had included a pack of cigarettes. The trucker was thoroughly pleased and grateful. He told me that, for quite a while, he thought this state sure had some funny people in it. I told him that everyone wasn't like that bunch up at Clines Corners.

He thanked me for stopping and told me to relay to Phil that he would never forget his kind handout, and would stop and thank him personally on the way back. He also said he would mention the Club Cafe to every driver he talked to. I'm quite sure that he also would mention Clines Corners. Phil was a large fellow with a heart as big as his body and just couldn't keep from helping the down and out. You'd better get up early, if you try to put something over on him, though. Thank you, Phil.

BAD BUS ACCIDENT AT
HYDRO, OKLAHOMA

The bus business is very seasonal, and sometimes the passenger loads are quite heavy. This was the case the night I was called to be the fourth section on the 10:05 p.m. schedule from Amarillo to Oklahoma City. Before leaving Amarillo, the regular driver (boss of the schedule) usually give instructions to the other driver or drivers on which towns to make and which ones to by-pass. This was to make sure that no passengers were left at any station. I recall that from Amarillo to Clinton, the third section and I, being number four, did what we called "leap-frogging." That's when one driver agreed to stop at a designated town and the other to proceed to the next, and so forth. This would allow all buses to have a better chance of arriving on time, or as close as possible.

This particular night, I was told to go ahead from Clinton and proceed to Weatherford just a few miles away. The other three buses would pass through and go on to El Reno. As it was early in the morning, and the station was closed, I was parked at the curb when the other three buses passed on through. I noticed the second section was now leading. Back then, the old Route 66 was a very narrow, concrete road, with curbs on both sides, especially up and down the hills, and only a single lane. We were beginning to get into the hill country, making passing very difficult.

About twelve miles out of Weatherford, and about two miles west of Hydro, there was a very narrow bridge, only about fifty feet long, with sides of heavy steel beams. As I came over the hill, I observed two buses parked as close as possible to the side of the road, as the shoulder on the road was very narrow. The buses' signal lights were flashing, and the third driver had thrown out some flares. After parking behind these buses, the driver told me that driver number two had had an accident and the bus was lying on its side in the bottom of a twenty-five or thirty-foot creek bed. He thought that some of the occupants of a car were also down there.

I could hardly put words to the feeling I had, the fear for those people--utter fear and disbelief, for I had just waved at that driver about fifteen minutes before. After instructing my passengers to please remain on the bus because, if they got off on their own, their insurance would be void, I worked myself down the embankment. I noticed driver number one at the front of the wrecked bus trying to evaluate the situation. He advised me that a motorist had gone to the small town of Hydro to notify the authorities. I'll skip the bloody details and tell the facts as best as I can.

The bus had been fully loaded with thirty-seven people. There were four people lying out on the bank who were assumed to have been killed on impact, as they went through the windshield. The driver remained in his seat, even though we didn't have seat belts back then. I think it was the steering wheel and dash that kept him there. He was conscious and talked to us during the ordeal. There was a lot of screaming from the passengers inside, and it seemed out of nowhere, truckers, other motorists, and probably a lot of local people arrived at the scene.

People began to swarm all over the right side of the bus, which was up and began prying out windows and lifting out the people. Even though the bus was diesel, I could smell gasoline. We later concluded that it was from the small gasoline engine that powered the air conditioner. Luckily, the fuel ran into the small stream that helped carry it away. I'm sure the people inside were terrified just thinking about the possibility of a fire or explosion. Oddly enough, the rescue workers didn't let that slow them down; probably it spurred them on. By the time the first passengers were removed, ambulances were arriving from both directions. There were now several law officers also on the scene.

During all of this, there was a young man lying on the ground screaming for someone to please help him; not for himself, but he needed to see about his wife and baby who were also lying out in the creek bed. Not knowing who made the decision that his wife and baby were dead, we kept telling the poor fellow that we were not qualified to move a person who obviously had a broken back. It turned out that this young man was driving his wife and baby eastbound, with a trailer in tow, when the faster bus came over the hill behind him. Somehow, they had gotten together, and we think the bus driver might have chosen to take the creek rather than to force his way through the bridge and perhaps hit the steel side with the bus. This was what all the other drivers thought, and the driver, not knowing the depth of the creek, which was misleading because of bushes along the bank and around the bridge, made a bad call. The bus driver was the last to be removed as the steering wheel was holding him in and had to be torn away before he could be taken to the hospital. The bus driver finally returned to the job after a lengthy sick leave, but had a crushed hip that caused a permanent limp.

It seemed like an eternity before I got back on the roadway and to my own bus. We were preparing to continue the trip when the wreckage had been cleared. Suddenly, a little boy on the bus started screaming. His mother and I found that he had gone to sleep and his left hand had slipped down beside the cushion. One of his fingers was caught in a hole about half an inch in diameter. The harder he pulled, the harder it stuck; then he would panic, and pull harder. While his mother tried to calm him down, I went to the rear of the bus where several young men were seated and asked if any of them had any hair oil, which was popular in those days. One of the boys handed me a small bottle of red hair oil. I poured a generous amount on his arm, letting it run down to his fingers and his hand slipped smoothly out.

At that time, we didn't have restrooms, so as soon as I got going again, we stopped at Hinton Junction at an all-night truck stop and gave the passengers a rest. Washing my face and hands the best I could, I noticed that my uniform hardly had a clean thread on it, but I got most of the oil and dirt off my hands. After leaving there, it was only a short distance to the Canadian River, which had a very long bridge across it. The bridge was wide and you could proceed at a high rate of speed, but it seemed I couldn't get the bus over about thirty miles per hour. The accident ordeal would probably match some WW II battle experiences that left me completely exhausted and depressed.

Until Interstate 40 was opened along old Route 66 years later, every time I crossed that bridge, I couldn't help but wonder how many other people were still living who would never forget that accident either.

In April of 1990, I returned to a little service station that's still open for business about one mile west of Hydro on that stretch of old Route 66 and talked with Lucille Hamons, whose father built the station way back when she was a little girl. She told me that after the bus accident, the bus was pulled up behind their old station and remained there until proper equipment could transport it back to Amarillo. My family and I drove another mile west and noticed that the old steel mesh that was damaged in the accident still remains as it has been all these years. Lucille also told me to notice the natural gas pipe line serving Hydro crossing above the creek. It's still there and it gives me chills to think of what could have happened if the bus had ruptured it. It's very hard to realize, when something like this is happening, that it could have been a lot worse than six dead (two in the car and four on the bus).

Drive carefully, and if you're over Hydro way, drive west on the old road and say hello to Lucille. You won't regret it. She will fill you in on a lot of history about old Route 66.

CAN'T TELL BY LOOKING

After completing a run, I was in the dispatch office when a bus arrived from Albuquerque. The driver rushed into the office to inform the dispatcher that he had an elderly man on board who needed immediate attention. The police were called and the old gentleman was taken off the bus and straight to the emergency room of a local hospital.

After the bus had left Albuquerque, the gentleman started talking to himself and creating sort of a disturbance. The driver, with the help of some other passengers, was successful in getting him settled down, at least temporarily. After leaving Tucumcari, the old fellow started acting up again.

This time, he struck some passengers and started becoming fairly violent. With the help of a couple of big fellows from Oklahoma, who volunteered to sit next to and behind him, they were successful in getting him to Amarillo where he was removed from the bus.

After the man had been taken away in an ambulance, the dispatcher went aboard and asked the passengers if the gentleman had any personal belongings. Some ladies said they didn't think he had anything. The dispatcher continued looking in the over-head rack and soon discovered an old worn, greasy, dirty, paper sack. He held it way out in front of him with two fingers and asked if anyone owned it. Naturally, they denied ownership; in fact, everyone thought it was trash. It seemed rather strange that they couldn't find anything else belonging to the old man, as he had started his trip in California. The dispatcher was obligated to investigate, so holding the sack a safe distance from him, he took it into his office and emptied it out on a table. Everyone present was sure surprised when over twenty-five thousand dollars in green bills fell out. In shocked disbelief, the dispatcher immediately called the police.

Several days later, the police finally located the old man's daughter back in California, and she could not believe it. It seemed that the old man had been committed to a home, with his assets frozen. How he'd obtained this sum of money was a mystery to her. The strangest thing, however, was how he traveled that far with so much cash in a brown paper sack! And, isn't it odd that no one claimed any knowledge of it when asked? You just can't tell by lookin'.

NO ANTI-FREEZE

Working an extra-board means that when you get to the first position on the board, you are obligated to stay by the phone so as not to miss an assignment. As I was preparing to go to bed one winter night, I noted that the wind was blowing hard and the snow was beginning to drift fairly high. I knew that I would be called for something before morning. Sure enough, the phone rang before I even got to bed and I was requested to report to the station.

Having snow tires on my old work car, I had little trouble getting to town. The dispatcher told me to go to the shop and, for the next eight hours, start

197

the eight buses that were stored there and keep them running all night. At that time, we were using the shop of another company and, therefore, had no personnel to take care of stored buses on a twenty-four hour basis. Also, Greyhound was one of the few companies that used no anti-freeze. It was probably cheaper that way, as most of the buses were either on the road or in a shop and all drivers were instructed, in case of a road failure, to cut the radiator hoses before leaving the bus unattended.

Proceeding to the shop, I was successful in starting all eight buses and setting the rpm at about six hundred. I returned to the station for coffee. I was feeling a little relieved that I didn't have to go on the road tonight, as the storm was really howling. About every hour, I stopped by the shop to check the revs on the herd. In between, I took drivers to hotels, picked up some, took them by an all-night restaurant, and generally ran a company taxi service till morning. I drove several grateful employees to and from their destinations, helped start several cars--anything to have something to do.

After arriving home the next morning, I wondered just how many cups of coffee one guy could hold during one snowy night in the Texas Panhandle, since every grateful person I had hauled just had to buy me a cup. After all, it was cold outside!

RACING THE BABY

One night, about fifteen miles west of Shamrock, I was going to Oklahoma City in an old gasoline-powered bus. Drivers had nicknamed this model bus "Dive-Bomber" or "9-90," because it would not go uphill very well but would literally scream going down. In other words, it would go uphill at nine mph and come down at ninety mph.

The bus was fully loaded, and through the rear-view mirror, I could see some of the passengers helping a young lady lie down on the rear seat. One of the passengers came forward and told me that the young lady was in labor and she was afraid she would deliver at any time. The lady asked me to see if anyone on the bus had any experience along these lines. My inquiry was to no avail and the young lady began screaming, quite loudly at times. Some lady was trying to comfort her as best she could. It seemed that most of the passengers were either cowboy-types, really elderly, or young sailors fresh out of boot camp.

The terrain was fairly hilly through this stretch of old Route 66 and, luckily, the road to Shamrock was mostly downhill. I decided that now was the time to see if this old dive-bomber could live up to its reputation. The first hill down proved the old girl was stout and true; the speedometer hand hit the peg at eighty and we hadn't gotten wound up good, yet. The highway, at that time, was only single lane. I couldn't help but worry about slow-moving traffic, for the brakes in those days were not all that good.

The good Lord knew that, so He kept everything out of the way. As I sat there, stiff as a board, my foot felt like it was sticking out the front of the bus. I got to thinking, "Good grief, of all the things they taught us in drivers' school, this sure as heck wasn't one of them!" I thought an umbilical cord was something you aired up a tire with, and the only surgical equipment aboard included a fire ax, my rusty old pocket knife, and a fire-extinguisher that wouldn't be of any use that I could think of.

The louder the girl screamed, the harder I pushed on the go-pedal. The hospital in Shamrock was only one block from the bus station. I don't even remember coming into town, but I recall, upon arrival at the station, jumping out of the bus and asking someone to call somebody, pronto. It turned out that the ambulance did arrive before the baby did.

While we were having a rest stop, an old cowboy-looking fellow commented to me that of all the riding he'd done, he thought this was the fastest. He thought we made the last fifteen miles in about ten minutes. This I never bothered to check, but I was sure proud of that old dive-bomber. I wondered for the rest of the trip why that rough ride on the back seat didn't go ahead and pop that baby out, but I was sure glad Mother Nature doesn't necessarily work in that manner. When I came back the next day, the lady at the bus station told me that the mother and blue-eyed baby girl were doing fine and her family was on the way out from Missouri to pick them up.

From that point on, every time an expectant mother boarded the bus, I asked her if she was sure that's what she wanted to do. For the next twenty-eight years of driving, I lucked out; I never had to be a baby doctor. If that had happened again, it would be me lying on the back seat, screaming and the expectant mother trying to revive me.

THE WINO

One cold evening about midnight, I was told
to go to the shop, pick up a certain bus, come to the
station, and load up for Oklahoma City. As one bus
was already loaded, I guessed I was sort of in a
hurry. At that time, we kept our buses in a
somewhat sleazy part of town, where it was not
unusual to see bums walking around at all hours.
Aware of this, I always had a good, heavy-duty
flashlight and my tire-bumping hammer in my hand
as I found the right-numbered bus.

Getting in the bus and starting it, I turned on
as many lights as possible and walked to the rear of
the bus to inspect the windows, seats, and floor to

make sure everything was okay. While the air pressure was building up, I went out to check all the marker lights, taillights, headlights, and to bump the rear tires with the hammer to make sure they were up. Returning to the driver's seat, I turned out the interior lights and prepared to back out of the parking space. The shop had a roof over the parking area, and was surrounded by tin buildings, so the noise was fairly loud. Getting backed out and preparing to move forward, I stopped dead when a hand touched my shoulder and a rough voice said, "Hey, Buddy."

Not remembering just what I did or said first, I know the second thing I did was to shove the flashlight in his eyes and back him down the aisle with my hammer in my hand. To say I was startled would be putting it mildly. It turned out that the guy was just a poor, old wino who had been sleeping in the overhead rack, and as I walked back to the rear of the bus earlier, I hadn't seen him in the rack above. After some pretty fast talking, he convinced me that he was homeless and that this was the only place he had to sleep. The last I saw of him, he was shuffling down the street, kinda' muttering something that I didn't care to know.

The lesson there was to check the overhead racks when inspecting the interior of the bus. On the way to the station, I got to wondering if he had an extra drink he would give a fella.

THE RED LIGHT AND WHITE LIE

One afternoon, as I was walking from the El
Fidel Hotel in Albuquerque to the bus station, I
noticed the temperature was very hot. I figured it to
be at least 100 degrees and couldn't help but wonder
what shape my bus would be in today. The bus I was
to take back to Amarillo was a through-bus from Los
Angeles to New York, and my portion was a 288 mile
stretch across the eastern half of New Mexico to
about the center of the Texas Panhandle. Our
biggest hill on this run was the one leaving
Albuquerque. It climbed fairly steadily for about
eighteen miles, topping out at the summit, Comers
Station.

We had been having a lot of overheating problems this year, and I wondered why, because Greyhound had already converted the forty-three passenger double-decker Scenicruiser by replacing the two small V-6 engines with a large V-8. Everyone had hoped the problem was solved. This was not the case, however. It seemed it was an everyday occurrence to battle the overheating problem. My thinking, along with the other drivers, was that this might be the fault of the transmission since it was only a four-speed. When the engine would be lugging between fifty and sixty mph, we were unable to shift to a lower gear until the speed came down to below fifty.

We thought the engine was straining excessively, causing it to overheat, but this did little to influence Greyhound engineers. We even told them that eighteen wheel trucks had eight cylinders and eighteen possible gear selections, pointing out that they never had overheating problems. But, no one could hear us.

This particular day, the driver who brought the bus from Flagstaff assured me that this old girl was no different. She sure had the "hots" as he called it. The engine was equipped with an automatic buzzer and red light on the dash indicating that if it was allowed to get any hotter, the automatic cut-off would activate and stop the fuel supply to the engine, thus saving a very expensive engine from burning up. We were so disgusted with the situation that we'd open the rear-engine door, and with gloves on, pull the wire loose from the shut-off valve and continue driving. This was, of course, reason for immediate dismissal, but gloves leave no fingerprints and I have never heard of a case where anyone was ever fired over this practice.

It was never known just what the company expected of us. If this was not done, we would have up to forty-three passengers sitting in the very hot bus while waiting for the engine to cool. The chance of getting another fourth of a mile before it happened again was very remote. At that rate, it would take approximately three and a half days to get out of the canyon. Sure enough, just as we were entering Tijeras Canyon, east of Albuquerque , the red light and tattle-tale buzzer came on. I decided to try going a little farther, hoping the engine wouldn't cut off. Wrong. The engine jerked to a stop and I immediately parked. I went to the rear of the bus, opened the swing-out tail gates and located the wire. With my gloves on, I gave it a hefty jerk, then closed the doors, and returned to the driver's seat. I hit the starter and the engine bellowed as we pulled out and continued. I hoped that no one would say anything because I didn't care to explain my actions and I certainly didn't want the passengers to be anxious about riding a pile of junk.

It seemed I was wrong again. A lady who was seated directly behind me leaned forward and asked loudly, "Driver, what was that all about?" Sometimes, a little white lie can save a whole lot of unnecessary explaining. I asked her what she was referring to. She asked, "What were all those red lights and buzzer, and why did we stop?" I told her

207

the bus was equipped with a radio-telephone so the dispatcher could keep in touch with us, and when he rang, the engine automatically came to a stop because it might be an emergency. Delay was not desirable, and the phone was in the rear to assure us of privacy. The lady leaned back in her seat, relaxed, and seemed quite pleased with all this new technology. We continued on and made the rest of the trip on time. I was very thankful the engine made it.

While having our dinner stop at the Club Cafe in Santa Rosa, a truck driver approached me and said that he'd overheard the explanation about the engine, since he was seated nearby. He congratulated me on the fabrication, for he, of course, knew better. He told me he could never make a bus driver. When I asked him why not, he said, "I don't think I could lie fast enough." After a good laugh, I told him that if he revealed my secrets, he would wind up hitch-hiking.

He promised.

THE DANCING LADY

As I was having coffee during a rest stop in Shamrock, a west-bound driver arrived, and after commenting to me that anyone could be late, he told me this story.

Leaving Sayre, going west, he had noticed an arm outside the bus. Back then, the buses had small windows that could be opened half-way. Even though it was night, he could see the lady holding something out the window. As we had no PA systems then, he had to stop the bus to see what was going on. This was very much a safety violation and also very drafty for the other people.

It seems the lady's complaint was that a woman was dancing on top of the bus in her high heels, and it was such a bother to the other passengers that she was trying to offer her money, as a last resort, out the window of the bus. She thought if she could bribe the dancing lady the rest of them could get some sleep.

The driver knew that in the next town of Erick a night watchman usually sat in his car and waved at the drivers. After stopping and talking with him, they both went aboard the bus and convinced the lady that they had removed the dancer and sent her to jail. The driver said the passenger then fell asleep and had been sleeping peacefully ever since.

BLACK ICE CHRISTMAS

Just a few days before Christmas in Amarillo the weather was a wet drizzle. I was assigned to deadhead a bus to Oklahoma City behind the regular schedule, which was loaded to capacity with packages and baggage. This was a common practice before Christmas, as the package shipments would exceed the normal capacity of the bus. They would load the bus interior, as well, and send it on to the next division point. The bus I had was completely empty, but was needed desperately in Oklahoma City, and I was told to follow the loaded bus. Both buses were the large, multilevel models. We left Amarillo about nine p.m. and made fairly good time to the Oklahoma state line. We noticed that the drizzle had stopped, but since the temperature had dropped, it was turning to "black ice." Adding to the problems was a rather stiff wind blowing out of the north. The combination slowed our progress considerably. By the time we arrived in Sayre, we noticed that we had been meeting less traffic and no truck traffic at all.

This surely was not going to be a fun night, and since Greyhound would not allow its drivers to use CB radios, we could only guess about what was ahead. The drivers often griped about the lack of CB radios, often commenting that even bull-haulers had radios, but after all, they were hauling cows.

Proceeding east out of Sayre, we finally made it to Clinton. The station there was an all-night restaurant, but no truckers or drivers were there to give us information. We continued east after a quick meal, and the only traffic was an occasional patrol car.

Taking approximately an hour to get to Weatherford, still with no traffic, we saw only a police car sitting on a corner. About five miles out of town, traveling at twenty mph, suddenly a gust of wind hit me from the left, and I felt the old girl start drifting toward the right shoulder. I remember trying everything: accelerating, decelerating, braking slightly, power-braking, all to no avail. The steering wheel felt as if there was a jack under the front end. Everything I tried was absolutely useless, and since I had no one on board, I even tried yelling at the thing. The front finally came back to the left, but the rear, which was a lot heavier due to the engine being there, kept going to the right until the bus turned completely around. I could see my partner in my rear-view mirror and for a few seconds, I was going straight. But now, my headlights were taillights, and taillights make very poor headlights. I wondered if maybe I could back up the rest of the way.

Wrong! The old gal had a different idea. She continued sliding off the road on the right side and stuck the exhaust pipe into a barbed-wire fence where she rocked back and forth a couple of times and came to rest. Sitting there crossways to the road, with my headlights shining up, I was rather relieved that I hadn't hit anything solid, such as a concrete bridge. There was no actual damage to the bus; but Greyhound now had a large, roadside advertising sign!

Leaving the headlights on, hoping that I wouldn't have to sit there all night, I just got my jacket on and was gathering up a few things, when I noticed a patrol car parked on the highway in front of me. When I left the bus, I fell flat on my face in the ditch. I couldn't get any footing, so I tried crawling up the slope. Still not getting any foothold because the grass and weeds were so completely covered with ice, I didn't know who had coined the phrase, "slicker than a doorknob," but that said it all.

The patrolman slid across and got out on the right side. Reaching his hand out and being careful not to let go of the door, he pulled me up out of the ditch. We talked a few minutes and he suggested that I return to the bus, turn all the lights out, and lock it up. Since I had broken no laws, and the bus was far enough off the road to be safe, it was perfectly legal. He felt there was no need for emergency units to come to an empty bus, and I agreed.

The driver of the first bus had seen what happened. Also, seeing the patrolman stop, he waited for us. After I had secured the bus, the patrolman drove me up to the other bus and we all visited for a short time. He asked why we were out on the road on a night like this, since everyone else had shut down except him. We didn't know, except to figure the dispatcher was sitting in a nice warm office, probably reading <u>Playboy</u> and drinking coffee.

After a good laugh, we proceeded to El Reno and I could tell that the loaded bus had much better traction than the empty one. As we left El Reno, it started to sleet. Boy, what a welcome sight that was, as the sleet added traction to the black ice. Before long, we were tooling along to Oklahoma City at a breakneck speed of about thirty mph. Quite a night indeed!

PLENTY OF TIME FOR A BEER

It was late in the afternoon, one summer day in the early 60s and I had arrived in Moriarty, bound for Albuquerque, about ten minutes early almost fully loaded with a double-deck Scenicruiser. At that time, I would go off duty and another driver would continue on to Flagstaff.

The bus station at Moriarty was a small cafe on the right side of Route 66 at the east end of the small town. After checking the tires, I went inside to wait for the scheduled departure time and to check for passengers and express shipments. Inside the cafe, I noticed a young, scroungey couple seated in a booth, but didn't think anything of it. The lady at the cafe advised me they were waiting for the westbound bus and they hadn't purchase a ticket, yet.

When I inquired if they wanted to ride the bus, they told me yes. The girl purchased two tickets to Albuquerque. About that time, the hippy-looking dude asked me how long until I would be leaving. I told him that we needed to leave immediately. He then asked me if they had time to walk down the street and get a beer. Evidently, the answer I had just given him wasn't to his liking, for he told me they would see me down the street. He again asked me if they had time. This time, I tried to make it very clear by telling him that if they wanted a cold beer, they would have plenty of time...in fact, they would have all night long. This didn't seem to register either, so they walked west toward a bar about three blocks away. I walked to the bus and, after a moment or two, drove off. They had almost made it to the bar as I went by. They started running toward the highway, waving their arms and shouting like crazy.

Little did they know or care that we ran some fairly tight schedules, with direct connections in Albuquerque for Santa Fe and points north. If we arrived very much too late, the other buses would leave, causing some passengers several hours of unnecessary delays. Needless to say, not many drivers would wait for someone to walk down the street for a cold beer, and we certainly didn't offer curb service at local bars...that's why we had bus stations.

As I went by them, some lady, not realizing the situation called out, "Driver, there's some people out there doing a lot of waving. I think they want to catch the bus." Keeping my foot on the accelerator, I answered her, "Nah, these people out here in Moriarty are just friendly. They wave at us a lot." We arrived in Albuquerque on time, and I suppose the couple had their beer; at least, they had plenty of time for it.

THE CRICKET INVASION

Several years ago, Oklahoma City had an invasion of crickets. I don't remember the exact year, but I can recall arriving at the station, and the sidewalk was literally covered with crickets. I couldn't believe my eyes. While I was unloading the passengers, several porters were actually using scoops and large trash cans. to try and remove enough of them for passengers to get around. The sidewalks were black and slimy. Crickets were hanging all over the building and the windows, and everything exposed was covered with crickets. As I entered the station, I noticed that several people were desperately trying to mop up the cricket juice.

The coffee shop had an enormous job of trying to serve food. Walking to the hotel one block away was a nightmare of being careful not to slip on the black goop, which resembled crude oil. You couldn't walk without crunching crickets. Once in the hotel, I tried in vain to clean my shoes. The hotel had spread out strips of canvas through the lobby and in the elevator. Upon my arrival on the third floor, I didn't notice any crickets. I was relieved and thought it would be nice to get some sleep. But, after getting in bed, I heard a cricket somewhere in my room. Oh well, I thought, if they don't start crawling up my nose, I'll just forget them.

Later that night, on the return trip, the mess hadn't gotten any better. Needless to say, every bus that loaded passengers in Oklahoma City had its share of bug juice in the aisle. As I traveled west about thirty miles that night, I noticed other towns were also plagued by crickets, but not as badly as Oklahoma City. They completely disappeared by the time we got to Shamrock.

Probably, people who study this sort of thing know why and how often this is likely to happen. A wheat farmer from South Dakota told me that he had lost entire crops to grasshoppers, but he didn't know that Oklahoma was subject to cricket invasions of such magnitude. I thought this sort of thing was found only in the Old Testament.

After a few days, they were gone as suddenly as they had arrived, as if by order of the High Command. Who knows?

THE RACE IS ON

About 1974, Continental Trailways was a fairly fierce competitor of Greyhound. This story concerns a little game of a different type of competition. Continental had a schedule due out of Tucumcari on its way to Amarillo and points east at the same time as Greyhound. Through the years, we had gotten used to the idea of them having the fastest buses. One of their drivers outrunning me every night was something I had grown to expect.

We always left town together and would go six miles east to the railroad crossing where we were required to stop. Then the fellow would blink his lights at me and that's the last I saw of him. One day, leaving Albuquerque with a double-decker, I soon noticed the governor didn't seem to work properly, for I could go so fast that the hand on the speedometer would hit the peg at eighty mph and still build up speed.

It dawned on me that tonight old Paul was going to be surprised. After arriving in Tucumcari, Paul and I had coffee and, as usual, he started kidding me about keeping up. After listening to him for a while, I told him he had better "go high-life" the rear end of his ole' red bus, 'cause tonight I was gonna' push him halfway, then outrun him the other half.

Well, he thought I was spoofing. We left town as usual and when we left the tracks, he blinked his lights as he always did and took off to the east. Letting him go in front for about a mile, I let the old girl loose and caught him in no time, but I refused to pass. I would just crowd him and blink my lights for him to go on. Knowing he was scratching his head and surely getting frustrated, I began pushing eighty mph. We were about five miles out of the small town of San Jon and I noticed headlights approaching fairly fast from the rear. I slowed down considerably and stayed at the legal limit, just in case. The car passed me and, sure enough, it was the "bogey-man."

The patrolman didn't bother me, but followed Paul through San Jon at a fairly high rate of speed. After clearing town, I noticed his red lights came on and he pulled Paul over. Easing on through, tiptoeing at the legal speed limit, I couldn't help chuckling about Paul. I thought the patrolman would surely let me go; I, at least, slowed down when I noticed him coming. Wrong.

As I approached his unit, he motioned me over, as well. Poor me. It didn't seem so funny now. He seemed to be a very nice guy. He just gave us a good tongue lashing. He said that, further back, we were pulling the fence posts out of the ground as we passed. We behaved ourselves then, until we got to Texas and we started the race all over again. Just before getting to Amarillo, I passed him, blinked my lights and went on down the road.

HOW MANY FINGERS?

Late one evening, I was the sixth section from Amarillo to Oklahoma City. It was just before Christmas and the passenger traffic was very heavy. The first section, which is the boss over the other six sections, was about thirty minutes in front of me and the driver had left word at Clinton for me to make everything from there on in to Oklahoma City, assuming that I was the only remaining bus that had any empty seats available. As the loaded bus in front passed through Weatherford, the driver held up two fingers, letting the people know that another bus was following. I recall that when I arrived, there were about five people waiting, but most had about lost their patience. Let me explain.

225

Through the years, in a situation like this, it was found that it was better to wave at the waiting passengers rather than stop to tell them to catch the following bus. Otherwise, if a driver stopped, there would be other buses stopping behind him and all explaining the same situation. This would just confuse the impatient passengers, while making the buses late at the next terminal.

One of the lady passengers told me, after finally boarding my bus, that as they were standing there the first bus came through and the driver held up two fingers and roared on by. In a short time, bus number two arrived, he held up two fingers and roared on past. Then a few minutes later, number three did the same thing. By the time numbers four and five followed the same pattern, she had overhead a cowboy-type dude asking, "How many fingers did those drivers hold up? Maybe we're getting the wrong message." Then, lo and behold, I pulled up and stopped. After leaving town, I explained and they, of course, understood, but couldn't believe that many buses would go through their little town. I think the cowboy feller was kinda' relieved to find out the correct signal was, indeed, two fingers. Be friendly!

SALT WATER TREATMENT

Quite a few stories could be told about the old narrow bridge at Hoxie. As I recall, the old bridge was about 150 feet long and was probably wider than it seemed. It was probably quite adequate when it was built, accommodating model A Fords and vehicles of that era well; but, this was the 50s and the vehicles were much larger and faster, plus the volume on Route 66 had grown considerably, I'm sure. Some of the buses we had in the early 50s were made of steel, and aluminum. Stainless steel had not yet made its debut. This story is about the advantage of the old steel buses, at least for one particular driver.

First, let me explain that Greyhound required from the driver a written statement, witness slips from the passengers (and anyone else involved), and about seven pages of accident reports anytime an accident happened. The company would then evaluate this and put the result on your permanent driving record. The paperwork had to be foolproof.

This driver arrived in Amarillo one afternoon, with both marker lights on the right side missing. The dispatcher asked him if he knew anything about it. The lights were long and streamlined, and protruded out about two inches, but were screwed to the side of the bus as separate units. These lights were missing on the bus, wires were hanging out, and the holes were very rusty. The driver's story was that it was that way when he picked it up in Oklahoma City, and since it was dark, he hadn't seen and reported the damage. Since the trip was a dry one, and the bare spots were extremely rusty, the boss had no choice but to believe him.

Several weeks later, after the incident had faded into history, we found out that the driver and a trucker had found themselves on that old narrow bridge at the same time. As he was coming out of the bridge, the truck was not slowing down. The bus driver moved to the right a little too soon and lost both marker lights. Neither vehicle bothered to stop, and since the bus driver would have been in much trouble had he reported it properly, he got the bright idea to go by the ice plant in Sayre and get some salt brine and apply it to the bare metal, hoping that it would rust in the next three hours. It worked, for I saw the bus myself and, believe me, it was rusty.

As you can see, some companies are like the I.R.S.; they actually encourage lying and cheating, and probably don't know why. Back then, we received awards, and in some cases, actual cash for safety. So, naturally, when we heard about an older driver who got his forty-year driving award, younger drivers would ask, "How can a fellow do that?" Another driver hit the nail on the head when he answered, "He lied a lot!"

Remember the three monkeys?

A TRIBUTE TO A BIG
GRINNIN' OKIE

In the past, I've had the pleasure of knowing and working with a lot of older drivers for whom I have the deepest respect.   For some reason or another, some incidents happen to a person who makes a particular story stand out. This is one of those true stories.

When I started working, it was with this huge, grinning driver who lived in Oklahoma City. His name was Burt Horn, and when he grinned, his eyes would become narrow slits and a gold tooth would show very prominently. There was absolutely no doubt that he loved life and loved helping people.

He was the most gentle person I think I've ever known. We would always do a lot of kidding around in the drivers' room. Burt loved a good laugh. As he was about six feet four inches and I was only five feet and eight inches, I'd sometimes run up to him, hold out my left fist, and thumb my nose with my right thumb, and growl and sniff, while at the same time running round and round Burt with a little dance like a boxer. Of course, this would give every driver in the room a big laugh, because, obviously, he could have literally thumped me into the floor so hard someone would have had to chisel me out.

Of course, Burt knew that I was funnin' and I think he liked me because when I would follow him on his schedule, I would always try to work with him anyway I could. I knew when it was time to work and time to "cut up."

One night, I arrived in Clinton right behind Burt. He had a character on board his bus who was becoming quite obnoxious. Burt had warned him to settle down, but to no avail. So, upon arrival in Clinton, Burt got off with a baggage crank, which was kept in the pocket located by the front door. This was a metal tool about a foot long used back then to open baggage doors. It seemed that when the obnoxious man came off the bus, he started with a line of profanity, then pulled a hunting knife on Burt. I was not an eyewitness, but was told that the knife was knocked out of the man's hand and flew across the driveway. Then Burt lost his temper. He grabbed the man by the neck and ran him up the brick wall of the station with his feet actually dangling in the air. Then as Burt was just about to put the fellow away with the baggage crank, the station manager rushed out the door and called out his name.

"Burt Horn! Burt Horn! That won't do it. Please put the man down, he's going to jail anyway!" Well, it seems that Burt stopped just a split second before sending the man to his Waterloo. In fact, a cop asked this guy, as he was putting the cuffs on him, "Sir, do you have any idea how close you came to walking through the Pearly Gates?" By the expression on his face, the guy would not forget this big, soft-spoken, grinnin' Okie. Would you believe, by the time Burt reloaded after the rest stop, he was GRINNIN' AGAIN.

HANK FINDS A JACK

One night, as I was approaching Clines Corners driving a double-deck Scenicruiser bound for Albuquerque, I began to notice a vibration in the bus. I proceeded a short distance and pulled off of old Route 66 into the gravel driveway, staying quite a distance from the gasoline pumps, so as not to interfere with their normal business. Clines Corners was a commercial agent for Greyhound, Continental Trailways, and New Mexico Transportation Company out of Roswell. I always thought we had a good working relationship with them. However, I found out this was not exactly the truth.

I stopped and stepped to the rear of the bus to check the eight tires for a flat. Bumping the tires with my old, faithful ticket punch, I listened for the ripe-watermelon sound that indicates adequate air pressure, also watching the punch for a rebound. If the tire is flat, the sound will be a dull thud ånd the tool will not rebound--like hitting on cotton. Every commercial driver probably has his own way of explaining flats. Another reason for inspection of dual tires is the likelihood of fire if the flat goes too long.

Well, wouldn't you know! The third tire I bumped, I got the old, sick signal that the inside rear tire was indeed flat. I then started the long, hard task of changing the tire. The spare tire and jacks are located behind the front bumper on most buses. While lowering the bumper, I wondered what I would do if the spare was flat. Luckily, I found it okay, and after getting all the blocks and the jack, I proceeded to jack the bus up. Poor old me, that jack wouldn't do a thing. I knew the service station had floor jacks, but only one night attendant that sold gas, etc.

Going in the station, I asked the young man if I could borrow a floor jack. His reply was that they didn't have any. As I could see one back in the bay area, I found his answer hard to believe. Asking him again if he was sure and telling him that I would gladly pay for the use of it, he again told me they had no jacks.

Returning to the rear of the bus, I wondered, "Now what?" In a short time, another bus pulled in behind me. It was the bus from Roswell to Albuquerque and was being driven by a fellow I'll call Hank. The reason I'll call him that is because Hank is actually his real name. He's over six feet tall with broad shoulders and one of the broadest grins I've ever seen, and he always wore leather gloves while driving. Maybe Hank had a thing about gloves, or maybe he had sensitive hands, but gloves were his trademark. After explaining to Hank what I had just found out, he told me to get the tire tools ready...he would go into the station and get a jack.

With his arms swinging at his sides, with those leather gloves adding to his arm length, and taking long strides, he entered the station. The young attendant rose out of his chair only to be met by Hank's leather finger. I've no idea what they talked about, but almost immediately, the young man pointed to the service bay, showing Hank where the jack was located. Hank returned to my bus resembling a gorilla pulling an alligator by its tail. Upon his arrival, I asked him how he obtained the jack. With a wide grin, he told me, "Maybe I know how to 'splain things better than you!"

After about an hour, we had the tire changed, and as we were going back to return the jack, I asked Hank if I should offer to pay for its use. Hank told me of many times he had brought out parts, papers, and other things without charge to the station and to forget it. Of course, I couldn't resist, I just had to thank the young man for the jack assuring him that I wouldn't forget it. Thanks, Hank.

SEEING ELEPHANTS

The schedule that departed Amarillo for Albuquerque (or any destination, for that matter) late at night was nicknamed "Hoot-owl Run." As I've heard many times, the only thing awake out on old Route 66 in the middle of the night are bus drivers and hoot owls; and hoot owls, at least, get to sleep in the day time, and only the owls give a hoot. All joking aside, any commercial driver will tell you that staying awake at night is the biggest problem he has. Many stories have been told about seeing objects that did not exist.

One afternoon, a driver came into the Albuquerque drivers' room and was telling some of

239

the guys about seeing, out on the prairie at the top of Palma Hill, a circus truck that seemed to be having a little trouble getting an elephant aboard. Probably, he preferred the grass to the truck! Anyway, after the driver stopped at Clines Corners, he overheard some people talking about the circus truck that had broken down three days earlier while attempting to get to the top of the hill.

Evidently, the only option they had was to chain the critter to a large tree and leave him temporarily until the truck could be repaired. They left him food and water, and someone checked on him occasionally. They were probably not worried about someone stealing him.

There were about a dozen drivers sitting around at that time and I remember that four or five of these follows had driven these "hoot owl" runs and were quite relieved to find out the truth about the critter. Several of them had seen the elephant in the dark hours of the morning; but, since they had no witnesses, they were very reluctant to even mention it. Most of them were probably sure of what they had seen, but were taking no chances of being the butt of a lot of kidding...like, "Yeah, yeah, we know, next thing you'll tell us is that it's pink!"

They all decided to wait for someone else to mention it first. I'll leave it to your imagination as to the laughter and kidding that went on in the drivers' room that day. Most of us went out to load our buses with our eyes watering from laughter. In fact, it was difficult to hold a straight face, just thinking about this small demonstration of human nature. What a relief!

HIPPIE AND HIS DOG

One night about midnight, I was unloading quite a stack of newspapers. While my head was stuck in the baggage bin, a long-haired, bearded hippie-looking fellow walked up and tapped me on the back causing me to bump by head. I hadn't notice him till then, thinking I was alone. I asked him if I could be of assistance, and he asked me how much it would cost to ride to sunup. Thinking that he was referring to a small town, I told him I didn't know where it was. We had a small town in west Texas named Sundown, but I couldn't place Sunup. Putting it a different way, he told me he wanted to ride until the sun came up, wherever that might be.

I told him if he'd give me some money, when the sun came up, I'd stop and figure out what he owed me.

This seemed satisfactory with him. I told him to go on in and find a seat. Instead, he put two fingers in his mouth and emitted a very loud whistle and then hollered, "Come on, dawg." A long-haired collie came running up to him...to say goodbye, I thought. He took him by the collar and started inside with the old mutt. I said, "Whoa there, fella, you can't take animals on this bus unless you're legally blind; then a seeing-eye dog is okay, but obviously this is not the case."

The hippie then informed me how stupid he thought this law was, and I asked him if he'd ever known of a law that wasn't; but that's the way it was, nevertheless. Giving him back his money, I watched him and his dog take off down the road with him muttering to the animal, "Don't worry, girl, I won't leave you behind."

That made me think he was faithful to at least one of God's creatures: man's best friend.

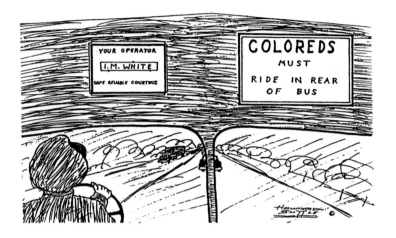

COLORED RIDE IN BACK

When I first started driving for Greyhound in 1951 at Amarillo, I was surprised to find that in the Greyhound stations there were two restaurants: one for "coloreds" and one for "whites;" there were also separate drinking fountains, and blacks were required by law, I suppose, to ride on the back seats of the buses. If that was not possible, they were to ride as close to the back as the seating would accommodate.

Reality hit home when I had to uphold these laws myself. I'm not sure exactly why it shocked me. I had grown up in the small, west Texas cotton town of Crosbyton, where I had gotten used to the colored people eating in the back of cafes and where they were required to sit in the balcony of the local theater.

As a kid, I remember we used to play with a colored boy by the name of George, but it never occurred to me then to wonder why he didn't go to our school. I probably was so dumb that I thought he didn't want to. He frequently came to our house, but I never knew where he lived.

The ignorance of the young is easy to excuse, but the prejudice of adults is hard to take...and even harder to have to enforce.

THE MIDNIGHT CRISIS

About midnight on a particular trip and, I was coming east into Santa Rosa, mentally going over the newspapers I would need to unload there. Anyone familiar with the hill west of town, it's easy to understand how fast an old Scenicruiser could sail down it. As I got to the bottom, it felt like the old gal was about to break the sound barrier, and all of a sudden from the upper deck, there was an awful commotion. It seemed someone was trying to kick the sides out of the bus. As no one was talking, I was sure it was not an altercation. Switching on the interior lights, I could see the legs of a large fellow protruding out from under the seats. Most of the passengers, awakened so suddenly, were also puzzled as to what was happening. Stopping the bus as soon as possible, I found the large fellow had had, in my opinion, an epileptic seizure. Having seen several in the past, I remembered the crucial thing to do was to protect the person from chewing or perhaps "swallowing" their tongue. The only thing I could think of to use as a tongue depressor was my plastic name plate, in a holder in the front of the bus.

The name plate was about one and a half inches wide and about eight inches long. Some other passengers were now involved and trying to help. We finally got the name plate inside his mouth and thought everything would be fine when, all of a sudden, he bit the thing in two. Working the pieces out of his mouth somehow, in desperation, I took my ticket punch, which I carried in a small leather holder on my belt, and worked that over his tongue. A couple of men held him down as best they could, and I headed on into town, about another mile or so.

As usual, the police were sitting around somewhere, and easily found. Blinking my lights at the police several times, I parked on the Club Cafe parking lot as fast as I could. The officer, seeing the fellow's predicament, called for more officers and an ambulance. We finally got the huge man into the ambulance, but it took about six of us to actually slide him down the aisle and onto a stretcher. The ambulance driver gave me back my punch and said that it had saved his life.

The Club Cafe was closed for business at this hour of the night, but Phil and Floyd had the night cleanup man let us in for coffee at any hour. After going inside and washing up, the night man got me a coffee can and water, and I boiled that old punch for about ten minutes. The next day, I swore there were marks on the punch that were not there the day before.

The next trip through Santa Rosa, Phil told me the man had depleted his medication, but after spending the remainder of the night in the hospital and receiving more medication, he had returned to normal and continued his trip. I was probably sure that the complications could not be transferred to another by saliva, but I still had to boil the punch.

In 1989, after writing to Jim Lehrer of the McNeil-Lehrer News Hour, we made a deal for him to have the old ticket punch, which he keeps in his Washington office, along with all sorts of bus memorabilia. His father was an old bus man and he is an avid admirer of the bus business.

THE NAVAJO AND THE RATTLER

One hot summer afternoon as I was on a run from Amarillo to Albuquerque, I approached the bus station in the small town of San Jon. Because the passenger flag was raised, I stopped and noticed that the waiting man was a short, fat, slightly drunk Navajo Indian. After letting the flag down and informing the "Chief" that he didn't need to ride the bus in his condition, the Indian showed me his left foot that had swollen to the size of a football and told me that he needed to go to the doctor in Tucumcari. After asking the obvious question about what had happened, the Indian showed me two fang marks right above the top of his untied shoe and merrily said, "Rattler."

Wondering if he would make it another thirty minutes, and because there was no doctor in San Jon, I felt that I had to let him ride. As he was hobbling on the bus, I told him not to do any war dances or chanting and that he had to be quiet. He responded, "Chief be quiet."

When we got to Tucumcari about thirty minutes later, I asked ol' Chief if he was going to the doctor now, and he said that he would go and immediately call the doctor.

About to drive off after a twenty minute rest stop, I noticed "Chief" still sitting at a table. I informed the owner of the restaurant of his situation, and when I returned the next day, he told me that after I left, the "Chief" had hobbled across the street to a liquor store. We laughingly suggested to each other that maybe liquor was the drunk man's doctor anyway. We could both picture the old rattler, after striking the Chief, gagging and falling over dead, or possibly wandering away drunk. In either case we had nothing but sympathy for the poor ol' rattler.

Can't you imagine some mother rattler telling her young, "Strike anything you like, but go way around them drunk Indians!"

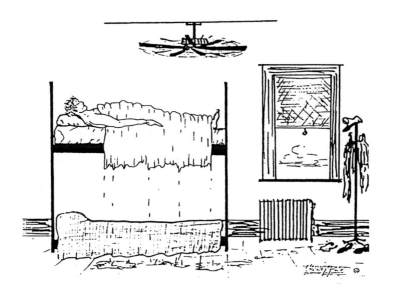

OLD HUDSON HOTEL

When I started driving in 1951, our place of rest in Oklahoma City was an old hotel one block east of the bus station. It was furnished by the company. Although we were union, it wasn't strong enough at that time to get us anything better. There were seven small half-beds in one large room, with one bath, and the only cooling was a ceiling fan. If you were lucky or tired enough, you might get to sleep a little during your eight hours off. Since it was a dormitory set-up, drivers were coming and going at all hours. During the summer months and at Christmas, the dorm was extra busy; but, at the slow season in winter, you could have more time there alone.

Once when I arrived in Oklahoma City in August about 4:00 pm, arriving at the hotel an hour later, I proceeded up to the dorm and took a shower. Finding myself alone, I had my choice of bunks so, naturally, I chose one directly under the old ceiling fan--which seemed rather comfortable for a few minutes. As soon as I had dried completely from taking a shower, I began to perspire. I must have dozed off a little. In less than an hour, I woke up and, at first, thought I had wet the bed; but, luckily, it wasn't that. It was just so hot and humid that the sheet I was lying on had become wet.

Knowing that I would be called to go to work at midnight and that the old 'hoot-owl' run to Amarillo was no picnic either, I had to get some sleep, somehow. I discovered that if I moved a little, the place where I hadn't been seemed rather cool. Then I hit upon an idea of taking a sheet off of one of the other beds and wetting it thoroughly in the shower. By rolling it around me, I managed to get some sleep that way. When I woke up about 8:00 pm, I repeated the process and somehow managed to get some more rest.

When the phone rang about 11:00 pm, it was the dispatcher telling me to go to work and, believe me, I was grateful for the assignment so I could leave the "comfort" of that old hotel. It's still hard to know how any of us managed to stay awake during those times, since tnere were many times we got very little sleep in such accommodations.

Another time I arrived at the dorm, it was bitterly cold. As I entered the room, I thought to myself, "I wonder why the last driver didn't leave the heat on?" Thinking it was a steam radiator, I opened the valve and could hear a hissing sound that I assumed was steam entering the radiator. After leaving the bathroom and preparing for bed, I noticed the strong odor of gas. At that time, I was a smoker, and I'm certainly glad I hadn't attempted to light up. After turning the valve off and opening the windows to air out the room, I figured out it was a gas heater and only resembled a steam radiator. After about thirty minutes, I could finally light a match and get some heat. As I lay there trying to go to sleep, I couldn't help but wonder: If I could make a mistake like that when cold sober, how long was it going to be before some drunk did the same thing and then passed out? I wondered how the old hotel had survived this long. Oh well, it wouldn't be long till I was back to the safety of the open road.

Finally, after several years of this, the company moved us across the street to the Black Hotel, and we were finally in an air-conditioned hotel. Then, a few years after that, we had a room with just two beds, which was really an improvement! To this day, I can't understand how the old-timers made it in Oklahoma City without air conditioning. Maybe they wrapped themselves in wet sheets!!

A BIG HUG FOR A LITTLE LADY

One morning while going east through Sayre,
I noticed a lady and small child at the small bus
station. This was probably a mother and daughter
going somewhere. As I finished unloading some
passengers, I motioned for them to step forward.
The mother told me that she would like to send her
five year old daughter to Hinton Junction, and her
parents (the child's grandparents) would be waiting.
This was a common practice back then. I assured
the mother that I would look after the little girl, and
would probably have a lot of fun along the way. The
child was dressed in what looked like an Easter
dress, real cute, with her patent leather handbag

and matching shoes with a small suitcase. The mother assured me that the little one had names and phone numbers with her. Putting the child on the front seat, as we usually did, made keeping an eye on her easier.

About an hour later, we had a lunch stop in Clinton, but the little girl said she wasn't hungry. After telling her that I would sure like her company, she joined everyone in the coffee shop. Noticing that the other ladies on the bus were very helpful in watching and helping with unattended children, this little lady was very outgoing and enjoyed the attention given her by several of the other passengers.

We arrived at Hinton Junction just about on time. The child noticed her grandparents' car and started to point, telling everyone that those people were her grandparents. As she got off the bus and finished with the huggin' and kissin' and so forth, the grandparents asked if she had been any trouble. I informed them that she hadn't been any trouble and had brightened up the whole day for everyone.

As they were walking off, I jokingly said to her, "Hey kid, how come everyone in the whole wide would gets a big hug but me?" She set her small bag down on the ground, looked up at her grandmother as if asking for approval, and when grandmother smiled and nodded, she gave me a real genuine bear hug. I told her, "Now that's better!" As they were driving off, she gave a big wave, and I think she felt ten feet tall for, after all, she had completed her first long-distance trip all by herself.

She probably remembered that first bus trip for a very long time. No telling how many of you people out there remember trips like that when you were a small child. Now, years later, we parents can't let our little ones walk home from school alone, much less take a bus trip. If this is progress, I sure wish we could go backwards for a ways.

A REAL LIVE PLUTO

It was just after day break, and I was "dive bombing," as we referred to driving in the hills of old Route 66 in the area of Hydro. It seemed that there was no one out there but me with an old 9-90 gasoline-powered bus this particular morning. Traffic was very light, and I was getting rather drowsy and looking for anything to do or things to see so I could stay awake.

Coming up over one of the hills and starting down the other side, the old bus would run very well, as long as its nose was pointed down. There was an old service station on the right side of the highway, closed of course, but I noticed an old bird dog cruising along at a good long gallop with his head held high. As he was also headed east, I came up on his rear. He reminded me of those old Pluto cartoons with his long ears floppin'.

Since I was going downhill, the old bus wasn't very noisy. With the engine in the rear, the dog probably hadn't heard me approaching. When I was about 200 yards behind him, I noticed his body leaning a little to the left, which gave me the impression that he was about to cross or enter the highway. Back then, we had a plunger valve located in the floor board, sorta' like a dimmer switch that was the air horn. I gave the button a good hefty push, and when that air horn went off about 100 yards from him, I have never seen so many legs on an animal in my life. He looked like a windmill wheel that had fallen off the tower, hitting the sand at a high rate of speed. He kicked up a cloud of dust that I could see through only occasionally.

As I passed, I caught the dog in my right mirror and he looked like he was tearing up Mother Earth trying to obtain some traction, for you could tell he was very anxious to proceed south to the next county, pronto! As I said, I guess I was getting sleepy and got the silly giggles. I got so tickled it was down right embarrassing. Most of the people were awakened by the horn, and not knowing what happened, were undoubtedly questioning the driver's sanity, for all they heard was the loud air horn and the driver laughing. I tried to disguise my laughing by coughing into my handkerchief At least I was awake. Maybe the good Lord put old Pluto out there for that reason. That sure taught me to be cautious: when feeling like you have the bull by the horns and the world belongs to you, look behind you. There may be some calamity about to blow you away, or at least scare the pee-waddlin' out of you.

So, when you get to feelin' cocky, remember old "Pluto," and how things can change in a hurry.

NO POWER-STEERING

One winter in Amarillo, the company elevated an employee to dispatcher. He was a nice young man, but much too gung-ho for most of the drivers. We thought that after he dried out a little behind the ears, he would be okay, Years later, he did turn out to be a very good man at the job. Not long after he started, however, he called me one very cold morning to come down to the office and correct a fifteen-minute mistake that I had made on the previous I.C.C. log. This was a daily record kept by the drivers showing hours driven, departure times, arrival times, etc. It was required by the Interstate Commerce Commission.

I tried, unsuccessfully, to explain to him that this was not critical and I would be glad to take care of it the next time I reported for duty. I drove through snow and ice to get the matter corrected. To add insult to injury, I was forced to make a written statement to the boss concerning this matter...I even had to endure his little speech about obeying government regulations!

A short time later, this fellow called me one evening to report to the shop. Upon arrival, I noticed a Scenicruiser in the shop fully loaded with passengers. The shop man told me to call the dispatcher. As there were about eight inches of snow on the ground, I wondered where I would be going. The young dispatcher was very congenial when I called. He informed me that the regular driver to Raton had gotten sick and couldn't report for work. No one could blame him. I felt kinda' sick myself and wondered if it wasn't a bit of "weather" sickness.

The dispatcher told me that I was the only man in town eligible to go this particular night. Then he lays it on me that this bus didn't have power-steering and it would be the next morning before the part to repair it would arrive. In his opinion, however, I wouldn't have any problem handling the bus. I couldn't help but think, here's a guy who makes such a big deal out of a pencil mark on a log-book with the gall to ask me to haul forty-three passengers through eight to twelve inches of snow on a double-decker bus with no power-steering. No way, José! He tried to pull rank, but to no avail. This fellow had never driven a bus and while sitting in a nice, warm office was telling me I wouldn't have any trouble.

After I quoted him almost verbatim about the importance of obeying I.C.C. laws, we waited until morning. Touché!

COFFEE SHOP

THE BIFOCALS

Called down for work one evening in
Oklahoma City, I arrived early, as usual, so I could
get some coffee and get awake. The dispatcher told
me that the older driver I was to follow and help was
in the coffee shop. Going inside, I found Harry
sitting at the large horseshoe shaped counter. I
noticed he was wearing rather large, dark-framed
eyeglasses. As I sat down and spoke to him, he
turned to me peering over the bifocals to get a better
look at who I was. He had gotten his first pair of
glasses the day before and was having a heck of a
time getting used to them. Having worn glasses
myself, I told him to just relax and use them, but to

try not to even think about them. As we were sitting there talking, a couple of long-haired guys walked in and behind us to get across the coffee shop.

This type of long hair for men was new to us back then, and they probably came from the West Coast, or perhaps from New York, where that was a fad. But here in Oklahoma City, it brought the following reaction, especially from a red-necked Okie like old Harry. He glanced around and, looking over and under his bifocals, said to me in a low voice, "Did you see that?" I said, "See what?" He answered, "Them two queer lookin' slobs with that long hair." I replied, "Yeah, and one of them even has an earring." I returned my attention to my coffee, but Harry just kept raving about what this old world was coming to.

About this time, I decided to pull a prank on old Harry, realizing that he was getting too serious. I said, "Harry, you can't tell by lookin'. I found out a couple of days ago that we have one driving into Oklahoma City." Harry looked over at me with his mouth open, trying to find me with his new glasses. He kinda' looked like a catfish in love. He said, "Aw, heck, you don't mean it?" I said, "Yep, that's right!" Harry then leaned over toward me and asked, "Who?" Turning to him and kinda' puckering my lips, I said, "Kiss me and I'll tell you." Old Harry's eyes got big, he took a deep breath, and in a very loud, husky voice, literally yelled at me, "Suttle, you no good so and so, I let you do it to me again! When am I ever going to learn to quit bitin' at this stuff?" All the time, he was slapping me on top of the head with his log book. He was talking so loud and mean that it was rather embarrassing to me. He had gotten the attention of everybody in the coffee shop.

For several years after that, every time I would see Harry and felt like kidding him a little, I would threaten him by saying, "Harry, if you don't do so and so, I swear, I'll kiss you in front of all the other drivers." This, of course, would get his goat, and he would reply something like, "If you ever try, you had better have plenty of salt and pepper to put on you ticket punch, because you're gonna' eat it." So, I was always very careful not to carry it too far...because I think old red-necked Harry was capable of doing just that. After that, I kept on the lookout for something that Harry would use on me to get even. It'll probably happen someday, too.

A CLOSE CALL

I had just left Erick, one rainy night, traveling east...when about two miles out of town, I met a vehicle that wouldn't dim its lights. This was not uncommon, by any means, especially on Route 66. It was probably due to a lot of people traveling long distances back then, or because of time, money, or perhaps some emergency. Flashing my lights up and down didn't get a response from the car, so I moved as far right as possible, and believe me, in those days that wasn't much (especially in Oklahoma)! Reducing speed, I hoped for the best, and as I feared, the vehicle veered across the center line in my direction. In desperation, I tried kicking the dimmer switch one last time, but to no avail. I then jerked the bus to the right, but it seemed the car almost went under my left foot.

Hearing a sharp thud, I saw, to my surprise that the car's tail lights were still on and we were okay. The car pulled off and stopped. I waved my flashlight for him to come back so I could talk with him and see what damage was done. We were several hundred yards apart at that time and suddenly the car just sped away. I looked the bus over, but I couldn't find any place he had come in contact with it.

I proceeded on to Clinton, where we had a rest stop and, while unloading baggage, I mentioned this to another driver. He took a look, and since the driveway lights were much brighter than my flashlight, he found a scrape across both sides of the outside rear tire and a small dent in the rim. On this particular model, the rear tires protruded out about one-half inch beyond the side of the bus.

The only thing I could remember about the vehicle was it appeared to have been a black sedan. Often since then, I have wondered how many people would have been hurt or killed had this fellow been over to his left a few more inches. Boy, I'll bet they changed drivers after that! Who knows what else needed changing!

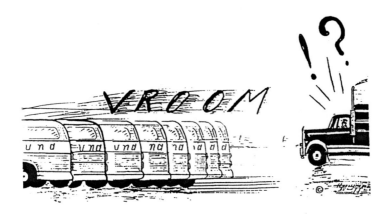

THE RUNAWAY ENGINE

One night, I was going east from Albuquerque
to Amarillo behind the first section driven by a big,
fat, jolly driver from Amarillo. This driver had been
with Greyhound several years before I started and
was a real joy to work with. As we left Tucumcari,
we were required to stop at a railroad track about six
miles east. Arriving at the crossing, I noticed that
the other driver's bus, which was a double-deck
Scenicruiser, was smoking so badly I couldn't even
see his marker lights. My first thought was that this
was a breakdown in the making and I wondered how
in the world we would get all those people on my
smaller bus.

273

As the smoke started fading away, I still couldn't see his tail lights, but by then the smoke had started getting farther and farther away, too. Thinking that I would find him parked along the side of the road at any time, I followed but never caught sight of him again. He simply disappeared into the darkness.

When I arrived in Amarillo about two hours later, and asked the dispatcher what had happened to the first section, he told me the bus arrived about thirty minutes ahead of time and the driver had already gone home. The driver told him that while leaving the railroad crossing about 106 miles back, he'd noticed the engine governor was not working and the engine was literally screaming. It was in the process of running away.

We had been taught back in drivers' school that all diesel engines have this potential. If this happens, the engine will keep building up speed until it literally flies apart, as some mechanic explained, and will just explode if allowed to continue unchecked. For that reason, all the buses had an emergency stop switch that would cut the fuel supply.

This driver, knowing what was happening, decided to let her go if she wanted to, trying to keep her in check with the brakes. It worked, because, according to the dispatcher, just as he came screaming into the drive, he flipped the stop switch and let the mechanic worry about it. Later, when I saw the driver, I asked him if he had had a speedy ride, and did he consider the highway patrol? He laughed and replied, "Heck, the highway patrol couldn't have caught me anyway, and couldn't have stopped me if he had!" Then he added that he was throwing so much smoke, he wouldn't have been found anyway. Finally, he admitted that he kinda' enjoyed it.

NO CLUTCH BUS

One morning I was called to report to the shop in Amarillo. After arriving and calling the dispatcher, I was assigned to take a bus to Dallas for major repairs. Finding the bus and beginning to get it started, I noticed the clutch pedal had been wired to the floor. Going back inside to ask Pete, the mechanic, what the problem was, he started laughing and informed me that the dispatcher had waited for me to get 'first up' on the extra-board to give me the assignment since I had more experience than some of the younger men. Pete told me that the bus had to be started in gear. As I started it, the ol' girl bucked like a one-legged mule and threw out a large cloud of white smoke. Pete was bending over in a huge belly laugh, and I've always thought that he had something to do with my getting that assignment. I decided I would surely pay him back provided, of course, that I returned from this trip.

The trip from Amarillo to Dallas wasn't all that bad as traffic was light, but as I entered Dallas on Harry Hines Boulevard, I was thinking this street should be called "Hairy Hinds" Boulevard. From that point on to the shop, which was located in the industrial section, was quite embarrassing. I couldn't time the traffic lights, so I would have to kill the engine, then put it in first gear, and when the light changed, I'd hit the starter button and start bucking like a bronc.

By the way people were staring, I'm sure they were wondering where Greyhound had gotten such an amateur. This turned out to be quite a workout for my left foot, and as I turned into the garage, I killed the engine for the last time. I looked down at the clutch and wondered how many times I had stomped on nothing but thin air.

Anyway, I swore old Pete had his "comeuppance" on the way.

THE DOMINO PLAYER

    I noticed while unloading my bus in Oklahoma City late one afternoon that some sort of ruckus had taken place inside the station. Not bothering to find out just then, I proceeded to the shop with my bus. When I returned to the station from the shop, I was told that a driver had had a little difficulty in getting an irate passenger's attention.

    The story starts with an old driver who lived in Tulsa and whose eyesight was failing fairly rapidly. I recall that he was a very small fellow who wore thick glasses, but was a prince of a gentleman. The people who had known him for years said they had never seen him lose his temper. He was on a run leaving Tulsa in the morning, with a two-hour layover in Oklahoma City, returning to Tulsa that same afternoon. Since his layover was only two hours, the company did not provide him with a room. This old driver would then sit in the drivers' room next to the bus station and play dominoes with anyone who might have a little time on their hands. It wasn't possible for anyone to beat him since he lived and breathed dominoes. He could literally tell his opponent what they had in their hands. He was so good-natured that everyone liked him. He had started way back and would, on occasion, tell some very interesting stories.

This particular day, when this old driver had arrived in Oklahoma City, there was a gentleman who was a lot bigger and very much younger giving him a hard time about something that happened back down the road. The dispatcher was called and he took the information from the passenger and advised him to leave the driver alone, that he would check out the complaint. The dispatcher also noted that the irate fellow had probably had a nip or two.

After the older driver had unloaded the passengers, he went inside to the ticket counter to help a lady with her ticket. Then, as usual, he was leaning up against the window sill of the bus station talking with a younger driver, who incidentally was also a club bouncer from El Reno, but certainly didn't look the part. He had red hair, was of medium build and seemed always to be smiling. He was a very nice guy and a close friend of the domino player. In the meantime, the irate passenger, finding some difficulty in getting the proper respect, returned to the older driver and started to curse and shove him around.

The red-headed fellow told the guy to please go away and leave this driver alone. This only brought on more profanity, so Red popped him on the chin, and according to witnesses, the fellow literally slid across the waxed floor of the bus station. This took the wind out of his sails for the moment, and everybody went on their way, rejoicing and thinking it was over.

After a couple of weeks, the red head was called on the carpet at the District Office in Tulsa. The boss told him that striking people might have been okay in the nightspots of El Reno, but certainly would not be tolerated at Greyhound. He instructed Red to talk to people, not hit them. After asking Red if he understood, the story goes that Red told the boss, "Yes Sir, I understand about talking, but I had to tap him slightly to get him to listen!"

The boss, of course, had no choice but to reprimand him on paper, but then they both headed out for coffee together. The boss, being an ex-driver himself, nudged Red on the elbow and asked him, "How far did you say he slid?" and after a good laugh, they departed.

Well, the domino player finally made it to retirement, with the help of all his friends, and I'll bet most of the time, you could find him shufflin' the bones, givin' you a big grin, and askin', "Got time for one?"

Good advice: don't pick on a smaller person. He may have a good friend.

THE OLD SILVERSIDE

One very hot summer afternoon in Oklahoma City, I was hanging around the bus station as an old Silverside bus pulled up to the dock. I asked the dispatcher if he was planning on running this pile of junk to Tulsa. He laughingly told me that the regular bus had broken down and this was the only bus he had right then. He felt that he must get some of the Tulsa passengers on the way at the regularly scheduled time. Silverside is the term the drivers used to describe this old relic, which back in its day was good equipment, but had become quite obsolete. It was equipped with a separate engine for the air conditioner and, as they were mostly worn out, you very seldom could get one running.

As the driver pulled into the dock on the sunny side of the station, I noticed that all the small sliding windows were open, proving that he had no air conditioning. Also, the old bus was leaning to the right and, of course, had no restroom. About that time a spiffy, new M.K.O. bus pulled up beside him. This bus was a competitor and it was an air-ride with an excellent air conditioner, restrooms, and tinted windows with a very plush interior. Both buses were due out about the same time to Tulsa, but M.K.O. arrived twenty minutes ahead of the Greyhound because he stayed on the Turnpike with no stops.

The driver of the Greyhound came into the station and told the dispatcher that at least he wouldn't have many people, because anyone with an ounce of brains would surely ride the newer, faster M.K.O. When the time came to get his call over the PA system, I've never seen so many people file out and line up at the old Silverside. He finally got loaded, and came in to inform the dispatcher that he had thirty-six passengers, with a seating capacity of thirty-seven. No one could believe it.

The M.K.O. driver got his call right after the Greyhound call, but he only got four or five passengers. Both drivers, the dispatcher and I couldn't believe what we had just witnessed. The Greyhound driver made the remark that he had better hit the road, because the only air they would get for the next two hours would be what he could stir up. The dispatcher and I got some coffee and we speculated that due to Greyhound's name being known nationwide, plus the fact that Greyhound was then running several national TV commercials, that advertising had made the difference.

Just goes to show, with enough publicity, you can sell anything.

THE UNHAPPY TRUCKER

Leaving Albuquerque at 8:30 a.m. on a through-bus from San Francisco to Atlanta, my run was to Amarillo with a rest stop at the Club Cafe in Santa Rosa at about 10:00 a.m. After the passengers had left the bus, I noticed a rather large, burly-looking fellow acting sort of impatient as I was parking. He approached me and told me flat out, "Boy, if you don't have my axle, I'm gonna get me a chunk of a bus driver. I've about had it with you guys. You're the eighth bus that's arrived from the west and all I get is the run around. I'm sick and tired of it!" Oh, boy. Poor me, what now? Checking my manifest and finding no freight for Santa Rosa, I listened to him explain again that he had called Albuquerque the day before and some parts distributor told him they would most certainly put an axle on the next eastbound bus.

Naturally, the trucker was getting impatient after waiting twenty-four hours and still no axle. His plight was not that unusual, for I had noticed back through the years, that most parts-counter men would promise the moon on the phone without checking if the part was indeed in stock. Or in some cases, if the part was available, for some reason, it would get sidetracked and wouldn't get to the bus station until the next day.

Calling our dispatcher in Albuquerque resulted in the information that the part had not been mishandled...in fact, it had not been brought in for shipment. The trucker was still unconvinced, so I suggested that he call the parts department in Albuquerque. Finding him a little reluctant to do so, I reminded him that he was standing out there accusing everyone of some sort of negligence, and now was the time to find out once and for all what the problem really was. He called and discovered that the dealer had the wrong part and had had to have the right one shipped out of Los Angeles, but it was due to arrive soon. They couldn't inform him of the problem as he was broken down on the road with no way to contact him.

He was very apologetic, and I told him that I understood his predicament, having had similar experiences myself. I couldn't help but ask him, "Sir, would you have really hit a guy like me who's so much smaller?" He grinned and shook my hand and replied, "Why, hell, no. You know I wouldn't!" We had a good laugh, finished our coffee and went our separate ways.

As I started up the hill going out of town, I certainly found it hard to take my teeth for granted.

POOR FAMILY AND
NO CREDIT CARD

One evening, while en route from Albuquerque to Amarillo, we arrived at the Club Cafe in Santa Rosa, for our evening meal stop. As the passengers were unloading and going into the cafe, I noticed a slightly unkempt woman, holding a small child, who was waiting to talk to me. I also noticed an old station wagon jacked up on the parking lot, as if it had broken down. The car was loaded with more kids and every conceivable household item that could be loaded, dragged, or tied on top. It reminded me that we don't have to go back to the 30s to see the "Grapes of Wrath."

This poor lady, looking tired and dirty, managed a smile as she exclaimed, "Boy, am I glad to see you!" Asking her if she was going on the bus, she told me that they were en route to Gallup, when the old car broke down. Their funds were depleted and it would take $200 to get the car going. It seemed the husband was moving them to Gallup because of family living there. The lady, in desperation, had called her father in Gallup and he was sending them a credit card on the bus so they could get the car fixed up and continue on their trip. The father told her to meet this schedule to get the credit card.

After checking the baggage manifest, I found no shipment or package for Santa Rosa. The poor lady was very disappointed, for they had been there in that old car for hours. Unloading the baggage bins, I looked for what had to be a rather small package, but found nothing. Feeling really sorry for her, I could do nothing about it. While inside eating, I mentioned her predicament to Phil, the owner, and he said that before going home after closing, he would make sure they had something to eat.

After arriving in Amarillo around midnight, while clearing my belongings off the dash of the bus, I moved an old shop rag that had been thrown there by the previous driver. Lo and behold, there in a flat envelope was the credit card for those poor people. Obviously the driver who picked it up in Gallup had the intention of keeping it on the dash so I would see it but, while the bus was being serviced in Albuquerque, the cleaning boy threw it farther behind the instrument panel and the rag had covered it up. I felt that, just like any bureaucracy, we had gotten so busy with our own little problems the we couldn't even deliver a small envelope. Now, that was efficiency.

The 12:30 a.m. schedule bound for Santa Rosa and Albuquerque was almost loaded. Taking the envelope to the driver, I asked him to please deliver it to that family. He would arrive in Santa Rosa about 3:00 a.m., which would be earlier than the mechanic could open his shop, so it would work out about the same as if I had delivered it. If Phil had given them food, I guessed it wasn't too bad after all.

The next evening, I noticed the old car was gone, and I wished them the best. I remembered that smiling face as she approached me expecting that small package. I wondered how far they had gotten.

THE STOWAWAY

The bus was a through, double-deck Scenicruiser from Los Angeles to New York City. Even though the bus would originate in Los Angeles, the passengers would not have to change to another bus the entire trip between these two points. The drivers, however, would change at what we called division points. Albuquerque was such a point, the next was Amarillo. This was my "run," as we called it.

This particular summer night, the passenger count was quite heavy, and I remember telling the dispatcher that I had forty-one adults and four children with the first passenger off in Santa Rosa, a distance of 118 miles. Although capacity of this type of bus was forty-three, the dispatcher decided to let me go without a second section as it would have been unreasonable to send another bus all the way to Amarillo and perhaps not need it.

I left the terminal by way of Central Avenue, which at that time was Route 66 all the way through Albuquerque, and everything seemed to be going quite smoothly. As I continued up through Tijeras Canyon, which at that time was a two-lane highway, it took considerable time grinding up Sedillo Hill. As I was approaching the summit, I noticed a small girl of about six years old coming up the aisle, continuing down the stairway, and I kept an eye on her, thinking she was going to the restroom located at the foot of the stairs on the lower deck. She kept coming forward and handed me a small, rolled-up piece of paper.

After the little girl returned to her seat beside her mother, I turned on the driver's reading light. I read a hand-scribbled note stating, "There's a man hiding behind rear seat." Thinking this couldn't be because of the lack of space, I, nevertheless, decided to stop at a truck stop about half a mile farther on and have a look. Stopping the bus, I turned on the interior lights and, taking my flashlight, I walked to the rear of the bus which had five seats across, all presently occupied. Stepping to the side, I asked all the passengers sitting there to exit the bus and wait by the door. The seats were designed so that each back could recline. Shining my flashlight over the top of the seats, nothing could be seen. Then shining my flashlight between two seats, I was somewhat shocked to see a large, black eyeball shining back at me. Releasing the seat back to the upright position, I could then see the man lying on his side in the small opening behind the seats in that area that would allow the seats to recline. Probably what had tipped the lady off was the painful grunt she could hear every time she tried to recline her seat.

I, with some persuasion, talked the man out of his position, which wasn't all that easy for him. After crawling over the other seats, I finally got him on his feet, escorted him outside into the lights and noticed that he was in his 20s, dark-skinned, with dark eyes and black beard. He didn't seem to understand English. It was my guess he was from one of the Persian Gulf countries. Asking him for his ticket, and getting only a blank stare, I then showed him a ticket. He finally said, "No." I asked him about money; he again said, "No." Having no choice but to leave him, I asked the passengers to re-board and take their original seats. As the passengers were returning to the bus, this chap tried to board with them. Catching his arm, I stood him back outside.

As I was closing the door, he started letting me have it in his native tongue, which I was certainly not familiar with. There was no doubt, judging by his expressions and hand movements that he was thoroughly disgusted with me. To put it plainly, he seemed "mad as hell." As I drove off, I was hoping he didn't have some kind of shootin' iron. After resuming the scheduled trip, I began to feel rather sorry for the guy. I also wondered if this dude had been riding there all the way from Los Angeles. He might have been, since none of the passengers had seen him before.

I couldn't blame the ladies who were sitting back there for being scared. It would be very hard to relax and get any sleep, knowing an eyeball was staring out at you from the cracks in the seats. Maybe this was normal in the country the stowaway came from, but I wouldn't know since I was unable to understand him.

But then again, maybe I did!

THE TICKET PUNCH

Some drivers carried their ticket punches in small leather holsters on their belts, and some just laid theirs on the dash. The punch was fairly large, a heavy chrome, hand-held tool used to punch holes in tickets for the purpose of cancellation. Each punch was designed to punch a different-shaped hole in the ticket. Each driver had his own personal punch and the design of the hole it produced was noted on our personnel records. This hand-held tool was used for many things, such as a small hammer, or to beat the rear tires to check for flats, or perhaps, in case of emergency, it could also be used for a club...or maybe even a tongue depressor. Most of the uses were not condoned by the company. This story is about one of those cases.

I was following a driver named Clarence Vaught one night on the old narrow Route 66. We had just pulled out of Santa Rosa heading west to Albuquerque. He had the double-deck Scenicruiser and I had a one-level bus. About ten miles out of Santa Rosa, a motorist came up behind me with his bright lights on, passed me, and caught up with the first bus. Regardless of what we did, he would not dim his lights. Since each of our rear-view mirrors on the buses was about ten inches square, the bright lights from a vehicle following close behind can become quite irritating. I tried to catch up with him and couldn't. I noticed that Clarence was getting quite annoyed, for he would blink his lights for the guy to pass. He pulled over, slowed down, but regardless of what he did, the guy was determined to follow him. To make matters worse, the car was fully loaded, which caused the lights to be even higher and, making the glare even more miserable.

As we approached Clines Corners, I assumed Clarence would pull over and stop, because it was a twenty-four hour truck stop and cafe. My assumption was correct, but to my surprise, the motorist pulled up behind the bus and stopped, also. He kept his bright lights on, and as I pulled up behind the car, I noticed Clarence walking back toward the car.

Clarence was a rather slender driver with a cool nature, and he was whistling as he passed in front of the car. It surprised me very much when he took out his ticket punch and proceeded to smash the right headlight of the driver's car. Still whistling, he went to the other side and knocked it out, too. Still whistling, he approached the driver's window and pointed the chrome-plated ticket punch at the man's face and told him that maybe, by the time he got his headlights replaced, he could understand the practice of common road courtesy and would dim his lights when following so close. This made me start wondering what I would do if the motorist started shooting.

Clarence then walked toward the coffee shop, swinging his punch and still whistling. As we were drinking our coffee, we noticed the motorist had driven over to the service station and was talking to the attendant.

We commented on the fact that the man would probably turn Clarence in to the company, but as far as I know, that didn't happen. Asking Clarence later if he had considered the potential consequences of such an act, he told me that after it happened, he did...but not before. He told me that he soon realized that a friendly talk with the man probably would have been sufficient, but laughingly said, "Oh well, they need to sell headlights, anyway."

We later learned the man had to wait until daylight to leave, as they didn't have his replacement bulbs. The man probably never failed to dim his lights after that.

Mark up another job well done for the old faithful ticket punch.

A SHORT NAP

It was during an airline strike one year that we couldn't even think about getting a day off. Seeing nothing but the center stripe and passengers had made me quite fatigued, because, for a family man, there are a few things that must be done during the short hours at home: haircuts, mowing the grass, etc. Plus the fact, this type of job required quite a bit of day-time sleeping, which will finally catch up with you. Even the neighbor's kids playing and dogs barking get to you.

This particular trip, I left Amarillo at 9:00 p.m. bound for Albuquerque, recalling that it was a tough battle getting part-way to Tucumcari. As I sat there having coffee, I couldn't help but envy truck drivers, who could pull over and catch a short nap anytime they felt like it. But, if your load consists of people, well, that's a different story. You can't even yawn without feeling like you're being watched. Poor me! Finishing the coffee and realizing that it wouldn't be long until daylight, I agreed with most drivers...the most difficult time to stay awake is at daybreak. After convincing myself to proceed, I arrived at the Club Cafe in Santa Rosa about an hour later. Knowing dawn was almost there and the rest of the trip to Albuquerque could be long and miserable with the sun coming up, I knew something had to be done.

After parking on the off-street lot, then opening up the engine compartment, I laid a rag on the ground nearby and put my flashlight on top of it. Then knocking on the cafe door, the night man let me in and, as usual, locked the door again. He asked if I wanted coffee, and I told him of my predicament. He laughed and directed me to the large, rear circular booth with instructions to take a nap, saying he would wake me in about thirty minutes. He said, if a passenger came to the door, he would simply ignore them.

That thirty minutes went by so fast I couldn't believe it. After telling me the time was up, he sold me a cup of coffee, and I returned to the bus. Sure enough, as expected, there was a male passenger standing out at the bus. He asked, "What in the hell is the hold-up?" I answered him as I started closing the engine doors, "Sir, we're about to enter the Great

American Desert out there, and as the engine was overheating slightly, I had to call ahead for instructions. I was told that it was okay to continue, but not to worry about waiting a few minutes if it would prevent a breakdown in no-man's land.

The passenger seemed quite pleased that I was that thoughtful and considerate of my passengers. Poor ole' me! This job could make a first-class liar of Saint Peter, himself. I couldn't tell him that I was inside taking a nap. Guess he was accustomed to having a three-man crew and flight attendants. This company wouldn't even allow us to have a transistor radio. Boy, I wished they would settle that airline strike. These folks started out mad and got more so every mile. Oh well, at least I felt somewhat refreshed. The guy went to sleep, and I went on my way rejoicing. It sure was nice to be able to see the road again, and I couldn't help but think, if passengers knew how tough it is for a driver to stay awake in these circumstances, they'd probably try to stay alert, too!

Greyhound Lines

WETBACKS TO EL PASO

On June 6, 1951, I was put on the extra board, which was the beginning of my seniority. The extra board meant we were on call most of the time and never knew exactly when and what the next assignment would be. About midnight one night, the dispatcher called me to show up at the station to take a bus load of wetbacks to El Paso. Since I couldn't afford but one car at the time, my wife took me down so she could keep the car. Arriving at the station, we were amazed to see about thirty-five scroungey, dirty, mean-lookin' dudes, known as Braceros. They were legitimate Mexican farm workers on their way back home. Generally, they were dressed in clothes that fit very loose, wore large dirty hats, had mustaches, and needed hair cuts. My wife asked, "My gosh, are you going to haul those characters?"

As it turned out, it was a fairly good trip. They were furnished sack lunches, and as there were no restrooms on the buses back then, I had to give rest stops at the side of the road. They would scatter like a bunch of quail and you could hear the barbed wire stretch as they would make their way to some bush...not for privacy, but to take advantage of anything that could be used in the place of toilet paper. After all, the paper sacks their lunches came in didn't last all that long.

The worst part of this trip was the odor inside of the bus which, of course, was not all their fault, considering almost every one of them smoked (Mexican) cigarettes, wore untreated-leather shoes or boots, and had not had the luxuries of even the simplest form of toilet articles, such as soap. This trip, like so many that I would make in the coming years, was a pleasure in the sense that they would always do what the driver suggested, there was no backtalk, no drinking, and plenty of gentlemanly behavior.

As I sat there, driving for the long hours, I often wondered how I would react under similar circumstances. I had to respect them for acting so respectfully to all the drivers. It seemed the cards were stacked against them. I wondered every time I put sugar on something if these men had harvested the sugar beets that produced it for me. I'll never know, but can thank them in my heart, anyway.

BAG NOT MINE

While driving on ole' Route 66 years ago, I was coming west through Sayre late one night. I stopped and unloaded a bundle of papers while a couple of ladies were getting out of their car. The little bus station was closed, but the lady had purchased her ticket previously. She was going to some place in California. I turned the inside lights on so she could find a seat and get settled, took her ticket, then (after she and the other lady did their good-bye huggin'), I noticed a large, brown metal suitcase sitting on the curb.

Feeling reasonably sure it was hers, but needing to be positive before checking it to

California, I stepped up into the bus as she was putting things in the overhead rack and said, "Excuse me, lady, but I need to know for sure if this brown bag out on the curb is yours."

The lady replied, "No, no, it's not. It belongs to my neighbor who lives about half a mile up the road from me. Her name is Martin, and she loaned it to me for the trip."

Thanking her, I noticed a few muffled giggles among the passengers. As I was loading her bag, I couldn't help but wonder how much better this country would be if everyone was as honest, especially politicians.

TUNNEL VISION

One night, as I reported for work in Oklahoma City, I found a very angry dispatcher on duty and noticed he was on the phone with the Oklahoma Highway Patrol. He later filled me in as to why he was so totally disgusted. It seemed that about three hours earlier he had called an Amarillo man down and had given him an assignment to deadhead an empty bus to Amarillo. He told the driver to go to the shop and get a certain-numbered bus, then return to the station and sign out before departing for Amarillo.

While the driver was in the process of getting his bus, another bus--a charter--was parked at the station's back lot. As the people on the chartered bus were eating, this driver arrived from the shop. The weather was fairly cold at that time, which only added to the mystery of what happened. The driver went inside the station, leaving the cold bus running, and signed out. He returned to the rear of the station, climbed aboard the chartered bus, backed out and left town, leaving his bag and coat in the cold bus. As the people finished eating, they returned to the bus, only to find out that all their belongings had been removed. Of course, the dispatcher was quick to discover that this driver had taken the wrong bus.

We were later wondering how this was possible, because the original bus was very cold, the charter bus was nice and warm with coats and belongings hanging out of the overhead racks. We couldn't believe that anyone could possibly mistake the two, and beside all that, before a driver even moves a bus, he adjusts the seat and rear-view mirrors. How could he get into a strange bus and have it feel right?

The dispatcher, with the help of the highway patrol, was finally successful in stopping the bus and sending it back. I can imagine what kind of reception that driver received when he returned to Oklahoma City. The passengers on the charter could only wait for their belongings, and had been at the station for a total of at least three hours.

As I recall, I think the only thing the driver received in the form of discipline was the nickname "Ole' Tunnel Vision." Until his dying day, he never outlived that name!

THE RUBBER UP-CHUCK

One day, the Oklahoma City dispatcher told me to deadhead on the cushions back to Amarillo because they were running out of drivers. I reported to the station and found that the two seats behind the driver were empty, so I put my bag in them so I could get on and off with the driver to help with baggage, papers, freight, etc. This was common practice among the drivers, but as the bus was being loaded, I noticed a lady move my bag into the overhead baggage rack and help herself to the seat. I stepped aboard and told her that the bag was there for a purpose and she had to obtain another seat. She was fairly upset because most older ladies love

313

the front seats and some of them will move anything that's not nailed down in order to sit there.

As we were on a schedule that made every little town and crossroads, I had to be careful at every stop to keep other passengers out of my seat. While unloading in Sayre, we were about five minutes "hot" (meaning ahead of time) so the other driver and I were looking at some of the typical bus station curios, or junk, if you please. When my friend spotted a flat rubber "up-chuck" that looked real enough to almost make you sick, he told me that's what I need to put in my seat to keep it reserved...if I had enough nerve to use it. I did.

After paying for it, we departed for Shamrock, which was a major rest stop. We usually had several passengers boarding there, plus quite a lot of baggage, too. After laying the rubber gimmick on the seat next to the aisle so it could be seen better, we had our rest stop. After telling my friend about it, he laughingly bet me that some little ole' lady would probably sit right on top of it.

As the driver started loading several passengers, I stood behind the door looking through a crack, watching the people. The first three or four people acted as if they didn't see it. Then two elderly ladies got on and I heard the one in front say, "Oh, look, Ethyl, there's two on the front." Thinking, "Oh, Oh. Here it comes!" I saw the next one start in, notice the mess, stand there a second, then pull Ethyl's arm and say, "Come on, come on, don't sit there." They proceeded to the back, and after loading the people, I stepped on as the driver was

314

closing baggage doors, and I sat right down, as if nothing was amiss. I couldn't see their faces from my point of view, but my friend told me those two ladies did a lot of whispering and pointing as we were leaving.

After we had gone several miles, I started reading a newspaper. While holding it with one hand, I slowly slid the rubber gimmick out from under me with the other hand and put it in my pocket. As we all disembarked in Amarillo, I felt that for the first and only time in my life, a couple of ladies were trying to get a good look at my rear end. I didn't allow them to do that.

This thin piece of rubber turned out to be the perfect solution to reserving a seat. They just couldn't understand how I could sit on it!

CAN'T GO HOME FOR CHRISTMAS

One Christmas Eve, most passengers were in a last-minute rush to get to their destination, but oddly enough, most were going east through Amarillo. Thus, I found myself headed for Oklahoma. Arriving at the Amarillo station, I found there were about five extra Amarillo drivers. Since I was the union chairman, I couldn't understand why we were stacking up like this. The other drivers told me there were three more upstairs. This made a total of nine men from Amarillo stuck away from home, and it was about 7:00 o'clock Christmas eve.

Normally, in years past, the company always let the drivers ride right back home on Christmas eve, because Christmas day itself was usually very slow and extra drivers were not needed. Also, by the time passenger traffic started picking up again, usually late in the day, Oklahoma City would have plenty of drivers. Add to these facts that it would cost the company more money for us to lay over, it didn't make sense to keep all of us men away from our families on Christmas day.

After a conference with the drivers, I went back to the dispatch office and found the supervisor was off until after Christmas. The dispatcher on duty seemed angry that he had to stay himself, so he was going to make us suffer, too. Trying to explain that the company and drivers had worked together satisfactorily in previous years only had him passing the buck, telling me he had his orders. Going into the baggage room where a phone was located, I called the union president, as was customary for the union chairman to do. His home was in Oklahoma City, and I found him there for the Christmas holidays. After explaining what was going on, he told me to return to the hotel, round up all the drivers, and show up at the station prepared to ride out on the 10:00 p.m. westbound.

He also told us to have our pay slips ready, because he felt sure that the cranky dispatcher would be more than happy to sign them, especially after he had made a call or two. He told us not to fear any backlash from this action, for he would be there to see us off. As all nine of us walked into the dispatch office, the fellow still held his ground. He asked me if we had decided to ride home on our own time, without pay...which then was half our driving wages. One driver said, "No, we're just waiting for you to reconsider!" The dispatcher answered, "That'll be the day!"

It was about 9:00 p.m. and we still had about an hour to kill before going home. Some of us were playing dominoes when our union president appeared on the scene. He went into the dispatch office, closed the door, and after a few minutes of talking, we noticed the dispatcher had called someone. He then got up from his desk and came into the drivers' room wearing a silly grin. "Well, fellows, I've changed my mind. My boss told me to send you home with pay!" He then authorized each man's pay slip, and we all wished him a Merry Christmas.

We arrived in Amarillo just about the same time as Santa Claus. In fact, I felt kinda' like Santa Claus, but I couldn't help but wonder if he ever had any trouble with a cranky dispatcher. HAPPY NEW YEAR!

THE BROKEN TOY

Departing Albuquerque at 3:30 p.m. eastbound to Amarillo, our first rest stop was the evening meal stop about 6:00 o'clock at the Club Cafe in Santa Rosa. We had barely gotten out of town when our attention was drawn to a small boy about three years old, sitting on the lower level with his mother. She had evidently just purchased a model Greyhound bus in Albuquerque. The toy, if pushed along, went on its own when released. Having no place to roll it, the child was scooting it across the seat to see how loud he could make it whine. Everyone was getting very irritated, except his mom, whom it didn't seem to bother at all. Subtle glances in the mirror had no effect, so I started thinking over my options.

If I tried to get her to quiet him down, and she told me she bought it in our gift shop, and that a kid playing with a toy was not a crime, then I would look like a fool. Then again, if I took it from him, his tantrum might be worse than the noise from the toy. Poor me. I had to figure out something, because the other passengers had the right to sleep, rest, and have a little peace. Finally, I had to admit I was stumped, so I decided to say nothing until I could get them in private at the rest stop. Realizing my options were few, I waited until everyone left the bus for the cafe. I walked through the bus to check on anything unusual like liquor bottles or passed-out drunks.

Passing the kid's seat, I saw he had left his bus behind. I could still hear the shrill siren of that cute little toy, and I could see the agonizing look on the other passengers' faces. So I did it. That's right. I gave that toy an attitude adjustment. I squeezed the rear wheels in such a way that the axle wouldn't turn--with the hope that neither he nor his mother could repair same. Then I laid it under a small pillow in his mother's seat and went inside the cafe to eat, hoping for the best.

As I entered the gift shop inside the Club Cafe, I couldn't help but notice some toy buses identical to the one he had. Praying that he wouldn't find out about his toy in time for his mom to buy him a new one, I sat down to eat. I couldn't help feeling guilty for conspiring against a three-year-old kid.

How childish, mean, dirty, sneaky, and deceiving! But, weighing that against listening to that whine for three more hours, I felt like a knight on a white horse.

After the rest stop, and as everyone was filing onto the bus, I was standing outside the door and heard the boy say, "Mommy, Mommy, you sat down on my bus and you broke it!" She actually had sat on it, and she told him how sorry she was. She promised to get him another one some place on down the line. I hoped it would be somewhere in Nova Scotia. As we started up the hill out of town, I could hear the little guy asking his mom what he was going to do now. She told him to read or look at a book. Glancing in the mirror, I noticed an elderly lady looking at me with a big smile on her face, and I wondered if she knew.

The next three hours were so very peaceful, and I noticed the little Greyhound driver had passed out with his thumb in his mouth. Probably bus drivers were this little guy's idols at the moment. Poor me. I had to quit thinking about it and enjoy the peace and quiet. "Leave the demolition to us."

MORE THAN A WOLF WHISTLE

It was a very hot summer day and my assignment was to drive a load of teenagers from Amarillo to Oklahoma City. I recall that the girls were all in shorts since it was so hot. There were two older ladies along as sponsors. We departed Amarillo about 10:00 a.m. and the trip was fairly normal until we were approaching the prison at El Reno. The older women, who were seated on the right front seat, asked me to pull into the prison parking lot, as they had plenty of time and had decided to tour the prison.

Not noticing this stop on my copy of the itinerary, I thought maybe I had overlooked it (I had been mistaken before!). Assuming that this group had made previous arrangements for the tour, I watched as the two older women took the entire group of girls into the administration offices. They were quickly met by two or three officials who hurriedly herded the whole pack back on the bus...amid whistles, yells, and hollers from the prison barracks.

After everyone got back on board, the officials stood in front of the bus and commenced to give these ladies a not-too-gentle lecture on the stupidity of unloading a group of young girls in shorts at, of all places, a prison! These men told us the place was full of prisoners who hadn't laid eyes on a pretty girl, especially clad in shorts, in several years. This would be about the best way they knew of to start a riot. The sponsors were informed that they would be welcome to tour the prison sometime at a later date, but would need to reserve time and certainly would have to abide by the dress code.

As I stood there thinking to myself that these two older ladies must feel really embarrassed, one official turned on me and told me to never (and he meant never) allow ladies to get off a bus at a prison dressed like that. He gave me the impression that his career would be enhanced if I never pulled another bus onto the parking lot. We reloaded and hit the highway.

After a few moments of quiet, I overheard a girl ask one of the sponsors if this is what she'd meant when she told them the tour would be educational. That broke the ice and I heard quite a bit of giggling for the next few miles. I would imagine that most of these young ladies never saw fit to tour a prison again.

THE ONE-EYED HORSE

Every so often, a passenger who's real
interesting will sit on the front seat...especially
interesting are the ones who tell their stories to
fellow passengers. But, there comes one every once
in a while, who every driver wishes they would do
one of three things: move to the rear, get off, or shut
up. One of those nights happened to me. The driver
who came in from Albuquerque told me about this
woman who sat alone on the right front seat and
would drive everyone around her crazy by quoting
the obvious--time and time again.

It was raining heavily when we left Amarillo
en route to Oklahoma City; and, as I recall, the bus

wasn't fully loaded--only about half full. It didn't take me long to figure out why no one else was sitting up front. As we pulled out of the station, a lady in the front remarked in her loud, squeaky voice, "Sure is wet out there, ain't it?" I tried to nod to her occasionally, but she was the type that you had to verbally acknowledge everything she said. I finally tried to ignore her, but to no avail. I tried to tell her that the rain and road made it difficult for me to hear her. She just talked louder. I even suggested that maybe she should get some sleep. She told me that she wasn't sleepy.

Driving on old narrow Route 66 in the rain didn't allow me much time to converse with her, but there are some who need to be entertained at the expense of the others who are trying to sleep. I was driven almost to the point of telling her that she must, simply put, shut up. About that time, we caught up with a pickup truck pulling a horse trailer somewhere close to Bridgeport Junction.

As I occasionally pulled up rather close in order to pass, she couldn't stand it any longer. She leaned forward in her seat and in her loud, screechy voice said, "My goodness, what's that in that trailer, the back end of a horse?" I tried to be subtle and tactful, but the urge came over me, and I said to her, "It's either the back end of a horse or it's just got one large eyeball."

To my surprise, most of the people were awake and got a good laugh; some even clapped their hands. After we got around the trailer, things began to settle down. I couldn't help but notice that she had cuddled up in the corner of her seat and didn't say another word all the way to Oklahoma City. I guess I found the only key that worked on her: she had been embarrassed. As we were unloading in Oklahoma City, another woman said to me, "I wish we had run across that "one-eyed" horse way back in Arizona.

The next time you are saddled with a compulsive talker, try embarrassing them. It may or may not work. At least, it's worth a try.

EL RENO, OKLA.

DEPARTURE   ARRIVING   TICKETS

TO   BUSES

HAMBURGER ETIQUETTE

The first section on the 5:30 p.m. from Oklahoma City to Amarillo and points west was fully loaded, so the first driver left instructions for me to make every stop between these two points, and he should see me at the dinner stop in Clinton.

There were several passengers getting off in El Reno. After loading a couple of others going west, a young man about twenty-five years old asked if he could have a word with me. He wore a black suit and tie, and looked a little out of place for the typical bus rider. He also seemed very nervous, so I took him back inside and sat down with him. He told me that he had just been released from the prison just outside of El Reno, and he was going somewhere in Colorado. The man's problem was that he had been in prison for several years, and he was afraid that he would do or say something that would brand him as an ex-con, and that he couldn't read too well, either. Seeing that the young man needed some help, I tried to put myself in his place, so I could be of more help. He stated that the prison had issued him the clothes, a bus ticket home, and a small amount of cash.

Advising him that I would be the driver to Amarillo where he would have to transfer, I told him that if he would do as I say, I would gladly help, and I didn't think he would be noticed by anyone. First, I had him remove his tie and coat, and get a newspaper. I suggested that he read or watch the countryside, relax and enjoy the ride. I reminded him that his debt was paid, and he was as good as any of us. He then began to relax, and I told him to wait and sit with me at the dinner stop in Clinton. I promised I would help him order something to eat, and would do so in a way that wouldn't be conspicuous.

He did everything I told him to. We had a good visit in Clinton, and I finally got him laughing a little. The remainder of the trip, I noticed he didn't sleep, but seemed to soak up the scenery of the country and towns along the way. I could imagine how the new-found freedom could be enjoyed. Upon arrival in Amarillo, I told him to go to the coffee shop and I would join him there as soon as I finished my duties. Before going, I sat with him for awhile and reassured him that he was doing fine. I tried to prepare him for the remainder of his trip, such as how to order food, etc.

A couple of days later, I checked with the Colorado driver and asked him how the prisoner did on his bus. The other driver then asked, "What prisoner?" He stated that he hadn't noticed anything out of the ordinary. Here's my wish, that he made it out in the real world. Maybe I helped a little.

THE WOULD-BE COWBOY

Late one afternoon, I loaded my bus and
pulled out of Amarillo for Albuquerque. About ten
miles outside of town, a man walked down from the
upper deck and approached the front of the bus.
After asking him if there was anything I could do for
him, I received no reply. The man just put both
hands on the dash and leaned over as if he was
looking for something. I asked again if he needed
anything; he looked at me, and I could tell by his eyes
there was "nobody at home." I immediately started
slowing the bus down in a gradual way, expecting
him to open the door and jump out. This had
happened before to other drivers, but never to me.
There's always a first time for everything.

The man, who was in his early twenties and fairly husky, would certainly have no trouble opening the door, as the handle was only inches from his hand. Glancing up in the passenger mirror, I saw a fellow looking at me and making a circular motion beside his head, which indicated to me that he had reason to believe the man's pilot light had gone out.

After concluding the man could be on some kind of drug, I decided to see if I could mention anything that might hold his attention. Noticing that cattle grazing out in pasture seemed to interest him, I asked him if he liked cattle. He then opened up and started talking about how all his life he had wanted to become a cowboy. I realized that if I could keep him talking for about fifteen more minutes, I'd be at a truck stop and could notify the sheriff.

Because Vega was a county seat, I started telling him that I knew a fellow in the next town who would be glad to help him get a job on a ranch. He seemed very pleased to hear this and appeared a little less nervous.

I asked him if he would like to get off with me, have some coffee in the cafe, and look around a little while I called my rancher friend. He nodded that he would like that. When we finally made it to town, the fellow and I got off the bus and went inside the cafe. I told the waitress what he wanted and gave her a little wink; she caught on very quickly. Then, as the fellow went to the rest room, I asked her to call the sheriff and kinda' fill him in.

When the would-be cowboy returned, I told him that a man would be by shortly who might be able to help him. Again, he seemed pleased.

After giving him back his ticket, we talked a while until the sheriff rolled up outside. I made my way to the door and asked the officer if he could manage the fellow.

He told me to go ahead and drive off, saying that he would probably let him sleep it off overnight and send him on his way later.

I never found out if the man was on drugs or just plain nuts, but one thing was for sure: a loaded bus is no place for a person with psychological or emotional problems like that.

After this episode was over, a man complimented me on the way I kept him talking about cowboys. I jokingly told him that I wasn't foolin'; if this guy could get a job as a cowboy, I would join him and ride off into the sunset. Happy trails!

THE BALLERINA

One night, as I was traveling between Santa Rosa and Albuquerque, westbound with a fully loaded Scenicruiser, fighting sleepiness and boredom in the wee hours of the morning, out of habit I checked the passenger mirror and thought I saw a ballerina dancing in the aisle. The law required every bus to have a night light in the rear of the bus that couldn't be turned out at night. It was also a requirement for all passengers to remain seated at all times while the bus was in motion, except when going to and from the restroom. This was, of course, to prevent injuries.

After a couple of minutes wondering if my mind was playing tricks on me, I took another look.

Sure enough, I was watching a woman in black tights and sharp-pointed shoes going through the motions that looked like a person shooing away flies from a picnic table after having eaten too much heavy, thick syrup...which had slowed her down to resemble slow motion while standing on ·red-hot coals.

After turning on the aisle lights, I had hoped to get her attention and motion for her to take a seat. Well, that didn't work, so I then was forced to use the PA system to ask her to be seated...all to no avail. Turning on all the lights, I asked her again. She continued to ignore my requests, so as a last resort, I stopped the bus and walked back to her and asked her to please be seated for safety reasons. She informed me that she was a member of some dance company and needed her exercise every so often. At this point, I was forced to inform her that I understood her predicament, and would be glad to let her out so she could practice her routine by moonlight--maybe a coyote howl might give her all the exercise requirements she desired. At which point, the very unhappy lady sat down and we continued on to Albuquerque.

At the station, I noticed the ballerina was the last one off and I assumed she planned it that way. She passed in front of me with her head held high and proceeded toward the station. Evidently feeling cheated out of revenge, she did an about face, walked up to me, stopped a short distance away, threw her head back, and looked me in the eye. Sharply she said, "Sir, you have a nose like an elephant's trunk!"

340

She then did a military about-face and strutted away, feeling a lot better about herself, I'm sure.

Thinking it didn't bother me, I noticed that...while brushing my teeth before going to bed...I often found myself inspecting my trunk in the mirror.

ABOUT THE AUTHOR

Howard Suttle was born and raised in the cotton and cattle country of West Texas and, except for service with the US Army in Europe during World War II, has spent his life in the wide open spaces of the Great Southwest. Howard was born just prior to the Great Depression and the Dust Bowl days of the 1930s, one of seven children of a pioneer Baptist preacher who died when Howard was ten years old.

Being the second oldest son meant awesome family responsibility. He picked cotton, "soda-jerked" in a drug store, was a movie projectionist, and held numerous other jobs to help the family survive. In World War II he was a tank commander for two years, until he was wounded and sent back stateside, where he married his hometown sweetheart and settled down to raise his own family.

In 1951, Howard went to Greyhound Driver School in Dallas, and drove from 1951 until 1979. His driving was largely done in Oklahoma, Texas and New Mexico along "old 66." He has traveled literally over two and a half million miles over the length and breadth of the Southwest during his twenty-eight years of Greyhound service, observing the land and its people, studying its colorful history, and putting to canvas the realism of everyday lives of the cowboy, Indian, the good times and the bad times, hardship and triumph of life in this often harsh and brutal environment.